T0197333

This Happens

This Happens

Roshonda Alexander

authorHOUSE®

AuthorHouse™
1663 Liberty Drive
Bloomington, IN 47403
www.authorhouse.com
Phone: 1 (800) 839-8640

Published by AuthorHouse 05/22/2015

ISBN: 978-1-4969-7332-0 (sc)
ISBN: 978-1-4969-7331-3 (e)

Library of Congress Control Number: 2015903508

Print information available on the last page.

Any people depicted in stock imagery provided by Thinkstock are models, and such images are being used for illustrative purposes only. Certain stock imagery © Thinkstock.

This book is printed on acid-free paper.

CONTENTS

Thank You vii

Acknowledgements..ix

Author's Note...xiii

Chapter 1 1

Chapter 2 5

Chapter 3 9

Chapter 4 13

Chapter 5 17

Chapter 6 21

Chapter 7 25

Chapter 8 29

Chapter 9 33

Chapter 10 37

Chapter 11 41

Chapter 12 45

Chapter 13 49

Chapter 14 53

Chapter 15 57

Chapter 16 61

Chapter 17 65

Chapter 18 71

Chapter 19 75

Chapter 20 79

Chapter 21 85

Chapter 22 89

Chapter 23 93

Chapter 24 97

Chapter 25 101

Chapter 26 105

Chapter 27 109

Chapter 28 113

Chapter 29 117

Chapter 30 121

Chapter 31 125

Chapter 32 129

Chapter 33 133

Chapter 34 137

Chapter 35 141

Chapter 36 145

Chapter 37 149

Chapter 38 153

Chapter 39 157

Chapter 40 161

Chapter 41 165

Chapter 42 169

About the Author 175

THANK YOU

Thank you for reading my book it is a honor for me to have been blessed to write this book, and share it with the world. Hoping that the writings of the contents found within this book polish the well intent of my heart.

This book was written to expose the occurrence of a life from the dark side of abuse and to help aid light for forgiveness, healing for the abused, and also the abuser.

For Booking
Roshonda Alexander
Post Office Box 240856
Montgomery, Alabama 36124
DROSHONDA@GMAIL.COM

ACKNOWLEDGEMENTS

For their steadfast love, belief, and encouragement the author wish to thank: God, her parents, and family. To her friends: Jimmy who showed compassion and belief in her, always being there when she needed someone to talk to. Tinita a graceful woman who is always pleasant to be in her company, being able to share her vision with, and she help polish it. Her children from the oldest to the youngest Savatore, Jada, Terrica, and Terrence Jr. I love you all unconditionally. Thank you for loving me, and praying for me, as I always say to you all we are bonded together for life. I'm a better woman because of all the storms that raged in my life, and God used it all to help better me. I have experienced the love, grace, and protection of God. He purposely added you all to my life to share life moments with, and to enjoy living the best life with you all.

This book is dedicated with love, and respect to God,
my children, my parents, and Grandparents.

To my friend,
In loving memory
D'Andre
Who blessed my life,
Whom we both were given a
Gift by God to be parents to
Savatore.
You will never be forgotten.

AUTHOR'S NOTE

The earth is the LORD'S, and all it contains,
the world, and those who dwell in it.
For he founded it upon the seas, and
established it upon the rivers.
It is beauty in it all.

CHAPTER 1

I believe everything has a beginning so I would like to begin this book with a strong foundation and that foundation is prayer so repeat these words, "thank you, God for allowing and blessing me to be able to have a copy of this book and give me the grace to read this entire book with your divine wisdom and understanding. I will be knowledgeable in the ways of you God and I will allow myself to be open to what you have to say to me through another person, to help encourage, inspire, challenge, motivate, uplift, renew, and to give me expecting hope with you God. I ask you to show yourself to me however you choose to and I will not run from you or hide myself from you. I ask that you shine and turn your face towards me every time I pick up and open this book to read because you are the foundational source and I will withdraw from all things and give you thanks and praise Amen."

The foundation has been laid and I must say that a strong foundation, is an unmovable and sure foundation that you will never have to give thought to and it will never fail you. God's word will never fail you, "God said heaven and earth shall pass away but my words will always remain." I believe God was saying, "I'm the God the creator who created heaven and the earth. I can do away with both and create again but my word is a gift to you who I am." You praise God and acknowledge him and you spoke to him through prayer concerning your life and relationship with him. Furthermore, in your future receive this written declaration. God is mindful of you because he has given thought to you and knows all about you. He gave deep thoughts of you before he created you and after he created you he spoke and declared eternal blessings over your life (Gen1chapter), so God declared blessings over you and the life he gave to you so it truly says that you are in a winning victorious outcome at all times. It is imperative that you see God in all things that concerns you and if you don't it will cause you to have doubt. God loves you! Question, do God know what is going on with you? Will he answer you, or will he manifest his goodness to you? It's like saying will God follow through faithfully, the answer to that thought and question is yes. Yes, God will and his purpose is to love you and for you to receive a relationship with him after all of what you have been through and out of that relationship you will receive the purpose he has for you that will fulfill your most inner joy to the fullest until it over flows.

The journey of Shun'boo, which was a young girl who grew up with her Stepfather, mother, four sisters, and two brothers. For a short period of time until she was removed from her home she was a very mature girl for her age in physical development. Shun'boo was a very pretty girl for her age and also she was very mature in speech and conversation which some would say she had a grown mouth but it was not so. Shun'boo understood right and wrong and had a lot of common sense. She would often cry because she felt set apart from others for some reason, such as her peers that were her age and she could not explain that question. She also could not answer why she exemplified great mannerism and she understood things very well that she saw more comprehensive than other children her age. She was a very clean girl as well as a caring young girl who always wanted to help those who got to know her. Shun'boo was a friend indeed. Shun'boo was a friend and a protector of all. The love of this young girl was amazing. She was a thinker and would often lay always thinking for the better and the greater to come and how she could live in that place of freedom. Yes! This young girl would think of these things as a child. She would often dream that she would be on a pathway walking and the path would seem clear but all of a sudden she would fall into the uninvited dark hole while feeling the gravity and the force pulling with weaken defense. She was not able to help her body from being pulled into this hole, and all of a sudden a powerful presence would come and catch her in the midst of falling.

She could feel the unseen force greater and mightier than that which was pulling her in this dark place, however, she would always want to see who that force was. She would be thinking who had wrapped their arms or whatever they had wrapped around her it was so much love, protection, and safety. In the presence of the moment she was elevated back to the path. Shun'boo also was very strong for her age. She was a strong minded young girl not easy at all to be persuaded of negative influences. She tend to have had a leaders' personality about herself. She was never afraid and furthermore she never appeared or showed it for others to see. If a challenge was for the better for what she loved she would do it. Yes, this young girl carrying the weight and burden of so much at a young age that was so unfair but never the less in her young mind she thought because she loved her family dearly she would do what it took to care and protect them. She was in love with her family and anything that associated itself with love. It was though it was the very thing that was concerning her well- being. She started working at a very early age. She was thirteen years young. She also started dating

CHAPTER 2

He said, "Hi" and begin to walk across the street approaching them as he was walking toward them. Her friend and sister begin to say how handsome and fine he was and Shun'boo was thinking while he walked across the street what did he want. However, while he was talking to Shun'boo friend she notice how gorgeous of a man he was and looked as though he was a well groomed gentlemen. He had said to Shun'boo friend, "excuse me but who is these two young ladies smiling with the most gorgeous smile which Shun'boo had seen while extending his hands towards them to shake Shun'boo and her sister hand they both introduced themselves politely. He shook Shun'boo hand last and held her hand a bit longer than he had held her sister's hand. Shun'boo said, "we got to get going because we got to get home because our mom is expecting us to be home at a certain time." He said, "Ok I understand. He replied, and asked Shun'boo for her phone number which she was so reluctant to give him the number because she knew her mom would respond in a disciplinary way that could be harsh at times. She said, "No" to him and her friend and sister said, "yes you can give him your number", while making all these flattering faces at him that cause him to laugh at them. Shun'boo asked him how old he was and he told her. Shun'boo was thinking he was too old for her so she gave him her number anyway. Drea said, "It was good seeing her friend and that he would call Shun'boo later on and for them to be safe walking home and to go straight home." Shun'boo thought silently to herself saying, "Who is he? Our dad."

Now, shaking her head at his words that he had just spoken while walking away from him still thinking how gorgeous he looked. Drea did call Shun'boo later on that evening and she waited close by the phone as often as she could so she could answer it if he called. However, she knew if her mom answered she would more than likely be in trouble with her mother as usual. Her siblings and she always had chores to do when returning home from school. She always had the most chores because she was the oldest and her mom was always so hard on her about everything. She always wanted to do everything right and correct it the first time when asked by her mother. She would do it right the first time so she would not get in trouble by her mom. Shun'boo was what one would call a perfectionist. Her mother was a clean woman as well but because of the many children she had she would allow them to do the majority of all the cleaning to the house. Her mother rarely worked outside the home and if she did it was only for a short period of time. Drea finally called and Shun'boo was able to answer the phone. His voice sounded so angelic on the phone. Yes, a young man's voice. He told Shun'boo that he wanted to meet her parents and to get there permission to date her. He ask so many direct question on what he wanted to know about her family and he sound as though he was trying to learn of Shun'boo's family. His conversation was quiet pleasing with laughter and throughout the conversation he had a great sense of humor. Shun'boo mom had come into the kitchen and saw her on the phone.

Shun'boo thought in her mind how she would have liked for a phone to be in her and her sister's bedroom because she could have had an excuse to lock the door and say she was changing clothes. Furthermore, even then she knew that she still would only have a short amount of time before her mom would come and ask, why is the door locked? Her mom didn't like the door shout and locked to long. Her mom would tell her to open the door but at least she could be far warned of her mom coming. Her mom asked, "who was she talking to, Shun'boo said, a friend she had meet coming from school and she said in a very high pitched voice. "Is it a boy"? Shun'boo, responded back "yes mama". She knew her mom was angry by her facial expression and tone in her voice and by that time her stepfather was walking in the door and they both could hear him coming in. Her mother said, for her to get off the phone and she would deal with her later. Shun'boo told Drea she had to get off the phone but he had already heard everything that was said between them. He asked her before hanging up what was her address. He said he would like to come over and visit this weekend after he got off work. That weekend he had called the house and her sister answered the phone.

He told her that he was on his way to their house and he said to her that he didn't know if he would call a taxi "which they called a cab where they live," or would he walk. However, he would be on his way so Shun'boo got up and begin to refresh herself up not even given thought to what her mother would say or what she would do. It was getting dark so she knew about the time he arrived it would be dark. She had brushed her teeth so long you would think she was brushing the enamel off. She combed her hair perfectly and applied vaseline to her body because they used that for a lot of things. Vaseline worked wonders to moisten the body and also a great moisten for your lips. Her siblings and her rarely got lotion or lip balm, "which they called lip chap." They

CHAPTER 3

He smiled at Shun'boo and said, "Hi" to her and he so gracefully and politely introduced himself to her mother and she could hear her younger sister saying how tall he was and how well dress he was and that he did not look all that. Shun'boo could hear them as her mom was asking him a lot of questions and he answered all them so polite he also had away with words. He used well- chosen words. He was very articulate. Shun'boo mom was very calm and she appeared to be somewhat impressed with this young gentleman, but here came the question. She asked, how old was he and he told her mom his age. Shun'boo mom said, "You know you are a bit older than her." He said, "Yes mama," that's why I wanted to meet you and her stepfather to get both of your approval to date her. Shun'boo mom stood there for at least a minute in a complete silence. Everyone was silent and you could hear the crickets outside. Drea was standing on the outside of the front door. Her mom said she would give some thought to him dating her daughter. Drea smiled and said, "Yes mama and thank you." He asked could Shun'boo come and sit on the front porch with him for a little while. Her mom agreed for thirty minutes and Shun'boo was so ecstatic that she was able to have some alone time with him because this was the first time she had seen someone who expressed and showed respectful, genuine interest in her. Shun'boo mom had the lights off the entire time in the living room. On the front porch the only light that was visible was from the television so his facial fixtures could not be seen completely as she had seen earlier in the week in the day light.

Shun'boo had thought Drea said yes mama a lot which was a good thing because to her mom it was one of the highest form of showing respect. "Saying yes mama was common in the south." Shun'boo went outside where Drea was as she was thinking I know he got to be tired if he had walked to her house as he had mention to her earlier. She did not know if he had walked or call a taxi so she asked him did he walk or call a taxi he said, he called a taxi. He said he didn't want to get there too late and it was the best choice. She agreed with him and they both laugh and begin chatting about how their day went. Shun'boo had told Drea she was on a punishment for giving him her number and talking with him on the phone. He said he was sorry and he believe that she was coming off her punishment. She asked him how he could be assured of that he said I think your mom would have ran me away by now. Shun'boo said, "Yes she would have," so that gave her a sense of ease about what her mom had thought and what she was thinking. He complemented her on how pleasant she looked and how pleasant she smell and she was thinking how she had use vaseline to moisten her body including her lips and that he had to be smelling the ivory bath soap she had use earlier that indeed lingered with her. It complemented her body chemistry and their chemistry was great as well. They both felt comfortable around each other just sitting a little distance of space between them as they sat there and talked she wanted to tell him how gorgeous he was but she kept it to herself.

She told him that it was near to their thirty minutes and she asked him how would he get home he said he was going to call a taxi back because it had got a bit late. They both heard Shun'boo mom say, "yes it is near thirty minutes and he could use the house phone to call a taxi." However, to their surprise Shun'boo mom was in the upstairs bedroom window. Shun'boo had wondered how long her mom was at the window listening to them talk. Her middle sister brought the cordless phone outside to call a taxi and Shun'boo asked her mom could she turn on the light so he could see how to dial the phone number. She said, "Yes" and when Shun'boo sister turn the lights on you could see Drea entire facial fixtures. He was stunning in beauty well manicured hands, perfect teeth perfectly position in his well formed mouth. He also had well formed lips. His clothes appeared as if he had just picked his clothes up from the cleaners and put them on. A great aroma that was coming from his entire body was a smell that was so pleasurable to the smelling senses, which could also cause anybody to enjoy his company. Besides all that he could hold a conversation. His taxi arrived and Drea said, he would call her in the morning gave her a hug as if it would be the last hug. Shun'boo had to stand on her tip-toes because he was much taller than her and he had to bend over so he would be able to give her an entire full hug. She immerged in his arms. Drea was hugging her as if he didn't want to let go so she started to pull back slowly he sealed it with a forehead kiss and a smile and off he left.

Shun'boo went in the house and her sisters and brothers was lying in the bed. They all appeared sleepy. Her youngest brother was asleep. The younger brother was only a couple of months young. Shun'boo took care of him as though he was her child. She was a natural caregiver at such a young age. She was a bit tired so she prepared for bed all though it took her a while to fall asleep. When morning arrived, awaken by

CHAPTER 4

She went upstairs to get dress hoping her mom didn't tell all of them they had to bathe together. All the girls had to bathe together except her youngest sister. She would have to take her bath alone and Shun'boo would be the one to bathe her and get her dress. That day her mom did not say anything about them having to bathe together so she was glad. After getting dress she came downstairs to the living room and her mom was sitting on the couch. She passed by her mom going into the kitchen to get some water and her mom asked, "What she was doing in the kitchen." She said, "I'm getting a glass of water." She said, "Make sure you wash the glass out and wipe the counter off." Shun'boo already knew what her mom would say. Her words would already be rehearsed in her head about what her mom would say and the consequences if she did not. She said, "Yes mama." She came out and her mom told her she was ready to talk to her. She stood there waiting with anticipation wondering what her mom would say. She said, "I want you to know that I was not pleased with you giving Drea the house number or anybody for that matter." She also said, "I'm going to let you talk to him as a friend. She asked her mom what that meant and she stated, "That means you can talk to him on the phone and you have thirty minutes to talk to him and he can come over on the weekend with my permission." She said, "You can go back upstairs now." She stated, "I will call you back down so you can go across the street to buy me a soda."

She said, "Yes mama," as she passed by her mom noticing how her mom would look at her the majority of the time as though she was always checking out her body and what Shun'boo was wearing. As she got passed her mom she said, "and don't think you are grown neither miss," which was one of her mom's favorite words to say when she spoke to her daughters. She use the word miss a lot when she was mad about anything or she just would say it. Shun'boo disliked that word. She had shared with her next to the oldest sister what her mom had said to her concerning Drea so her sister said you should call him and let him know what mom said. She said, "ok" and she waited for a while to go back downstairs so it would not be so noticeable to her mom that she was being anxious to call him which her mom would have called it being "hot." After some time had pass she went to get the phone and her mother had gone upstairs to her bedroom. She was in there with her stepfather with the door closed entirely so that meant for them not to knock on the door unless it was an emergency. She knew her mom would be in her bedroom for a while because she had come to know her mom and her stepfather patterns very well. They would be having sex "which her siblings and her would call it doing the nasty" because that's what her mom would say it was when she was talking to them about sex and explaining the nature and purpose of it. Her mom and stepfather would be a bit loud where her siblings and her could hear them clearly. Shun'boo would tell them to not pass by their room or she would turn the television up so her siblings and she wouldn't hear them. They all disliked the sit down talk about sex because she always made them feel as though they had done something that was inappropriate how they all would sit there so restless.

14

Shun'boo mind would wonder off thinking how many nights her mom would come in the room and take her hands and rub on them to see if they would respond. However, that's what her mom would say," I'm seeing if anybody have been touching on you all and if so how would you all would respond." Shun'boo would think how do we supposed to respond to such sick and perverse of such an act done to any child. She would think why her mother would not just ask them since she also had been touched by a family member already knowing how that will make a child feel. Shun'boo went and turn up the television because she could hear them but she was happy because this would give her more time to talk with Drea on the phone. She called him up and his mother answered the phone. She had a very distinct voice. Her tone and speech was slightly deep. She asked who was calling and yelled to him, "Drea a girl is on the phone for you." He answered within a couple of seconds. Shun'boo said, "Hi" and he said, "Hey I was thinking about you." She said, "Do you know who this is." He said," of course I remembered your voice from the very first time I met you and we introduce ourselves" He asked, "did her mom talk to her about him being able to date her?" She said, "Yes her mom did talk with her." You could hear the anxiousness in his voice to hear what her mom had decided. She told him that her mom had said that they could be friends and that she could talk to him on the phone and he could come over with permission.

He said that was great and at least she was allowing him talk to her and see her. They chatted for a while on the phone because Shun'boo mother was still occupied in her bedroom. She asked Drea if he could hold on for a minute because she thought she heard her baby brother crying. She walked over to the bottom of the stairs and could hear him crying. She said to Drea, I will have to call you back because my

CHAPTER 5

Shun'boo told her mom that his diaper had been changed and she was headed downstairs to prepare a bottle for him and before her mom shut her bedroom door she said and don't forget to burp him. She said, "Yes mama" and she went down stairs. By then Drea had called like he said he would. Shun'boo was glad he had called when she had just finish feeding and burping her brother. She just was sitting at the kitchen table holding him talking sweet making up baby words to her brother that he seem to enjoy. He would be smiling and as though he was laughing out loud. He was the most beautiful baby you could have seen, which at least to Shun'boo. She would always wait for him to get sleepy because he would yarn and she would always smell his baby breath it always smell clean and fresh like a scent that only babies have. Drea had said he had notice she was a very caring person who loved her sisters and brothers. He said he would get her mother permission to see her next weekend but in the meantime he would call her through the week. He asked where her stepfather was. She said he was at home at least for a while because he was a truck driver and her sisters and brothers rarely knew when he was leaving out unless her mom had spoken with him about something that she wanted him to punish them for. She told Drea she would call him back. She begin to think how the punishments she had endured were followed with unpleasant harsh words which followed with a whooping. However, for Shun'boo it would be a beating with deep embedded bruises but Shun'boo was a very hard girl who had to learn to never show weakness to her stepfather or mother.

She would stand or lay there and take whatever they did to her without any emotions being shown only a angry facial expression. Moreover, the anger only burned inside her because of her sisters and brothers would have to see their harsh acts and harsh words being implemented on her. She would think how unfair it was to have her siblings see their stepfather beating her that way and striking even harder because she would never cry nor shed a tear. She would not speak a word at that time. She would be thinking how she didn't want her siblings to be in the house when they were in a raged of such a harsh state towards her. She could hear her mom's voice saying to her stepfather hit her harder "hit her she think she is grown she want cry give her some to cry about" still she would never shed a tear or say a word. He would stop beating her when he got tired or if her sister would start crying yelling for them to stop. Yet, after all they would do to her she loved them both still especially her mom. She loved her with a love that was unexplainable. She would give her life for her mom. How could a girl of such young age think and feel and think such thoughts. She knew she was different than most children and girls her age. While other children were doing youthful things and activities or hobbies or sports or just playing, Shun'boo was taking care of her sisters and brothers. She knew how to care for them because it came natural to her. Drea had gotten her mom's permission to come over the following weekend to see Shun'boo.

She was hoping the week would go by fast because she didn't like going to school because she encountered many fights with her peers even a few fights was with boys. She was a fighter, very strong for a young girl and especially for her age. She never backed away from standing up for herself and her siblings. She showed no mercy when it came to them. She would think they would have to kill me before she would allow anyone to hurt them and she made that known to any of her peers who wanted to fight them. She would take on one or many which never seem to bother her. She was a protector of what she loved and she was a friend if you were her friend. That week she sat in the class room hoping that it would be a good week because her next to the oldest sister and her would have to fight often and it was mostly because of girls being jealous of her. Even much older girls who lived in all the same neighborhoods as they lived in, such as her present neighborhood. The week went well. Besides her teacher asking her why have she been falling asleep in class most of the time she had always been able to fight her sleep but she was a bit more tired than usual. However, it was her menstrual time and she always was a bit more tired at that time of the month. She explained to her teacher that she got more tired at that time of the month. Her teacher had told her that she might need to speak with her mom about taking her to the doctor to see if he could give her something to help her during that time of the month.

She didn't want her to fall asleep in class and miss class lecture that she would need for class. Shun'boo said, "yes mama." She also was thinking she was glad her teacher was a woman and she was thinking truthfully to herself how she was a bit tired from the many chores she had to do at home. Furthermore, school had come to the end of the week and without any fights she was looking forward to the weekend because she was expecting to see Drea so she begin preparing for him coming over to visit her. She cleaned up all the major things in the house so Saturday would be easy on her and she could have more time to take

CHAPTER 6

After getting a bath she was so tired she did not care about bathing with her sisters she was thinking how she just wanted to lay down and go to sleep. She was hoping she would lay down and just dose off right to sleep without having the dream that she would be on a path and suddenly she would fall in a dark hole that she would often have that night. She fell asleep and she heard her mom voice saying come and eat breakfast. She laid there thinking for a few minutes how she had slept through the night without having the dream that she would often have. She was happy and in a great mood which she never really was in a bad mood regardless of what had happen in all the previous dreams. She was always protected from falling in the dream but felt the power of love and that this force knew her. She could not explain. She would lay thinking after awakening from the dream what or who was that this greater force she did not know but would overwhelm her with protection. She got up brushed her teeth, washed her face, and made sure she had appropriate clothes on and went down stairs for breakfast. When she got downstairs there sat her sisters at the table almost done eating. Her mom told her to hurry up and eat because they had to clean up and get dress. Her mom's house had to be cleaned and cleaned up when she said it had to be done and it better be cleaned. She always did a cleaning check behind them. Shun'boo was thinking how she would wake them up out of their sleep at night and make them rewash the dishes and it could be extremely late sometimes.

How she would think often of a place where peace and rest was at and did it even exist. She told her mom that she had did majority of the cleaning on yesterday and she reminded her that Drea was coming over today. Her mom gave her this look of madness but did not say anything so she headed up stairs and started cleaning her bedroom that she shared with her sisters. She asked all them to help out with the kitchen because she didn't want to hear any arguing, such as who turn it was to wash dishes. She told them that Drea was coming over today. They all seem happy that he was coming over. They all agreed to clean the kitchen because they said they wanted to see him as well. They all finished working together and got the house clean and they made sure they cleaned well because they knew their mom would do a cleaning check. They all begin getting dress as time went by. Shun'boo was thinking that the house had to pass her mom cleaning inspection because she didn't call their names they made sure that the house was clean. Her stepfather was there so she was thinking would he meet Drea today as well. She was done getting dress and was waiting for Drea to call her within the hour. He call her and said he would be there. He said he would be there within the hour. He said that he was walking over her house. She said, ok be careful. He arrived about an hour. Shun'boo answered the door when he arrived. He was a gorgeous young man. She invited him in and as he was entering he had to duck his head just slightly because he was a tall young man.

He came in and asked Shun'boo for a hug and complemented her on how she looked. She wore some prefect fitted jeans and nice blouse.

Her hair was perfect, freshly smelling like ivory soap, and perfectly oil skin from the vaseline. With her toes and nails freshly manicured and pedicure by the one and only Shun'boo. She took great pride in taking care of her hands and feet. He also complemented how nice and clean the house was so she thought thinking he was an observer. Shun'boo was pleased to hear him compliment the house because her sisters and she had worked so hard to get it all done before he came over. They did not have the most lavish furniture but it was used furniture and kept up. He asked where everyone else was and where her parents were. By that time her stepfather had come downstairs and she had introduced them. Drea stood up to shake his hand and they began talking. Her stepfather said to Drea," you have some height on you and I like that necklace you have on." He said, "thank you." He asked him did he play any sports. Drea said, he played basketball and that started a conversation between them. Shun'boo said she was going upstairs to let her mom know he was downstairs and her stepfather said she already knew and she would be down in a minute because she was taking care of the baby. She told him she would be back down because she was going to get her sisters and brother so he could meet them. She went upstairs and told them that Drea was downstairs and her sister that was next to the oldest told her she already knew and she asked them did they want to come downstairs and meet him.

They all said, yes but her younger brother was not that enthusiastic about meeting him because he wanted to play with his toys. Her sisters and brother came downstairs to meet Drea. Her stepfather and Drea had stepped outside and she thought why they would go outside. She knew it had to be her stepfather suggestion and wondered what questions he would ask. However, she was at ease because she knew Drea would answer them truthfully and respectfully. It was as though it was his

CHAPTER 7

He handed it to her and said," I don't mind about doing it. She said no you are a guest. I will wash the glass. He smiled and said, "thank you." Her mom had come downstairs where they were. He was standing in the kitchen as her mom was walking towards the kitchen. He said, "Hello. How are you today?" In a murmuring voice she said she was doing well. It was barely where you could understand her. She told him to sit down she had to ask him some question so she begin to ask him a lot of questions. She asked him everything from who was his parents, what were their names, what did he do for a living, and did he finish school? She even asked him was he a virgin he laughed and she gave him that stare as to say "I'm not playing", and he knew it. He said, "No mama", there was complete silence in the room. Then she said well Shun'boo better be a virgin while she was looking back and forth at them both. Shun'boo said nothing following her mother's comment she was thinking in her mind she always think the worst of me. Her mom asked Drea how he got over there, he told her he had walked. He also told her he enjoyed walking and he told her it did not take him that long to walk from one place to the other than other people. He said he was a fast walker. Her mom said for her to keep an eye on her sisters and brother and for them to not go in and out the door. For her to not be acting grown "meaning fast or hot" that what she called it. She said, "Yes mama I'm not fast or hot."

Her mom said, "You heard what I said." Her mom headed back up stairs and Drea asked did they have a store nearby. She said, "Yes", they had two neighborhood stores that they would go to sometimes. He asked, "Did she want anything from the store." She said, "Yes" Drea said, let's go outside and ask your sisters and brother do they want anything. Drea and Shun'boo both walked outside and asked if they wanted to get something from the store and they said, "are you buying it," and he smiled and said yes. They said, "Sure we would like something," and Shun'boo, middle sister said. She wanted a burger and Shun'boo interrupted her and said no. Drea was speaking about a store where they sold chips, candy, and cookies, those type of things. She said, "Ok." Drea said, "I will take you all to this place I know you would like." He said it was located downtown. Then Drea said the name of the place. He asked them had they been there before and they all said no. Next, he asked what places they enjoyed to eat at and her sisters began to name some of the places that they enjoyed eating at. Shun'boo told Drea they don't eat out much that they only ate out a few times out of the year. She thought to herself it was always around Income tax time when they got a chance to eat out or get anything new from a department store. He said that was fine. He said I will take you all out to eat if your parents will be ok with me taking you all out. Shun'boo sisters just looked at each other. Shun'boo was thinking who was this guy.

He was gorgeous, he was polite, respectful, kind and thoughtful and not to mention always appeared to be so happy to see her. She felt peace when he was around. Drea asked Shun'boo to go get their parents so he could ask if all of them could walk to the store with him. Shun'boo thought she might let them go because all of them was going and besides she knew that she would protect her siblings. Shun'boo went upstairs and knocked on her stepfather and mom door and ask could she come downstairs because Drea wanted to ask could they all walk to the store with him. Her mother said go get him and tell him to come to the bottom of the stairs. Shun'boo went to go get Drea from outside and they both came back inside the house. Her mom was standing at the top of the stairs holding her baby brother in her arms. Shun'boo wanted to get him but she wanted to enjoy the company of Drea. Her mom asked Drea what he wanted and he replied, "can Shun'boo and her sisters and brother walk to the store with him so he could buy them some snacks." Her mom said, "Yes", but her brother and youngest sister could not go. She said for Shun'boo to go get them and bring them in the house and for her to fix her baby brother a bottle before they left. Shun'boo asked Drea to open the door and she walked out in front of him and told them that they could walk to the store with Drea and that her next to the youngest brother and youngest sister could not go. Drea took his large hand and placed it on their shoulders and ask them what they wanted from the store.

They told him what they wanted and he said ok smiling as always as he and Shun'boo walked them back inside the house. Drea said I will help you prepare the bottle for your baby brother if you show me and they both laughed and walked to the kitchen to prepare the bottle. She asked Drea has he ever tasted baby milk before. He said, "No." Shun'boo showed Drea how to prepare a bottle. She told him the final step was he had to taste it. He asked her if it was breast milk. She said, "Yes." Then he said if she could just taste it since she was a girl and it was her mother's breast milk. She started laughing and told him she was just kidding that they just had to squeeze a little on their hands to

CHAPTER 8

They shared with Drea how they had raced against each other and Shun'boo was wearing a blue jean skirt that day. When she asked her did she want to race she said yes and she said I asked Shun'boo did she want to go and change from her skirt to some shorts she said no. I'm going to keep my skirt on and win this race. Drea said "oh no!" As she was telling him she said we begin racing and she started out slow and I was in the lead and all of a sudden she by passed me. She was winning the race and she was coming upon a downward hill and she said I notice she was losing her balance and she fell down. When I got to Shun'boo, I asked her was she ok she said yes. As I helped her up, our other sisters came over as well to make sure she was ok. We all were brushing the dirt off her helping her walk back to the house. Our mom had come to the upstairs bedroom window the same window she was at when you first came over to our house asking us what were we doing and we told her that Shun'boo had fallen. While she and I were racing we helped her get back to the house. Our mom started yelling at us to just get in the house and yelled from the upstairs bedroom window at Shun'boo for wearing a skirt and racing. She was mad cursing at her. As we walked back with her Shun'boo fell out. Drea said she fell out. They said like unconscious. They all said, "Yes" and we all were around her yelling and calling her name and our mom was in the window.

She didn't come down to help us with her. She finally opened her eyes about a minute of being unconscious and we asked her was she ok she said, yes. As always she was the strong one and was trying to walk back to the house by herself. My other sister and I put our arm up under hers so she could put her weight on us as we walked her back home. Our mom was still in the window yelling and cursing that night as we all got our bath and got into bed. They told Shun'boo how scared they was when she had fell down unconscious as she laid in the center of the bed. We all laid around her and she said she was ok and that she loved us and she said I have a new created tooth in my mouth and they said what you are talking about. She said I chipped one of my front teeth while racing and they all was asking her to show it to them. When she showed it to them they said it's not bad. She just laughed she said to her next to the oldest sister, but it was bad for you to get in a race with someone who had a blue jean skirt on. We all started laughing. Drea started laughing and they were near the store. As they got ready to enter the store, Drea told them that they could get what they want. You would have thought Drea was a kid in a candy store because he had bought so much candy for himself. Shun'boo said, "Drea you have got so much candy you have enough to last for a week." Drea smiled and said, "Yea I do and I'm not sharing." She said," ok I don't want no part in getting cavities."

Shun'boo thought she would have cavities because her back teeth would bother her sometimes. Her siblings got what they wanted and they all walked to the register for Drea to pay for it. On their way back home Drea told them a crazy story but it was so funny it was as if Drea was making up the story. As he was telling them they all were laughing.

When they arrived back to the house they all went inside and sat in the living room and enjoyed their treats and talked. As evening was approaching Drea said that he was getting ready to leave Shun'boo told her sister that Drea was getting ready to leave and they all told Drea thank you for the treats and your funny story. Drea said, "You don't have to say thank you to me." I was happy. He asked if she could go get her parents so he could say bye as well. She went upstairs to knock on her stepfather and mom bedroom door. She really did not want to knock because she knew how her mom got when they knocked on the bedroom door, especially when the door was closed. She took a deep breath in and knocked on the bedroom door. Her mom said, "Yea what do you want?" She never asked who was at the door. She would say yea and waited to hear what they would say and then she would determine if it was important to have knocked on the door. Shun'boo said Drea wanted to say goodbye before he left. Her mom said tell him bye with no questions. Shun'boo went back downstairs and told Drea what her mom had said. He said, "Ok." He asked, Shun'boo to walk him to the door.

He said he was walking home. She told him to be careful and Drea gave Shun'boo a hug and said that he would be careful going home. He gave her a hug and a kiss on her forehead her sisters and her talked about what they thought of Drea, and she did not share with her sisters much about him she had her defense up because of how her stepfather treated her mother. She saw all levels of abuse that he had implemented upon her mother. She had so much resentment and how she viewed men in general. Drea began to visit often not just on weekends but through the weekdays as well. Drea started getting very close with Shun'boo. There was no doubt he really cared a lot for Shun'boo. Even though she enjoyed having Drea around it still was hard for her to accept opening up to Drea. She had somehow developed another dark place of defense.

CHAPTER 9

Drea not only took care of Shun'boo necessities of life. He was providing for her entire family often buying groceries for her family, clothes, and shoes for her sisters and brothers. Also buying school items, paying bills at her parents' house. It began to get overwhelming for Shun'boo that her parents where asking for this type of help from Drea. It was also a bit embarrassing, Drea had so much attraction towards her but never pressured her about anything. Shun'boo knowing that if she told Drea that she wanted to give her virginity to him that he would not turn her down even though he was respectful to her. Even respectful Drea would not forbid the chance if it was given. Drea and Shun'boo would talk a lot about a host of things. Drea was always giving and trying to take care of all of her issues that should have never been issues for her. This young child caring the burden of her siblings and her environment, there it was a little stability. Shun'boo mom started allowing her and Drea to leave for much longer periods of time together. They would walk or catch a taxi to the store, go shopping together, and many of those times was an opportunity for her to give Drea her virginity but they too would somehow keep it from going that far, at least Shun'boo did. Drea had talked to her about a job he thought he could get her that he said he knew definitely that he could get her that if she wanted it and if her stepfather and mom would agree to it that he would talk to the family about her working there. It was a family owned business.

Shun'boo was excited knowing that she had an opportunity to make money that she could use to take care of some of her needs as well as her siblings. She told Drea she would love the opportunity to work and ask him could he talk with her mom about her working. She asked him was they alright with her working after school and weekends. He said, "Yes" he had already discussed that with them. She was so excited she had jumped in Drea arms not realizing what she had did. She looked Drea in the eyes as he lowered her safely on her feet. She asked, Drea "why do he do the things he do for her?" He said, "Because I want the best for you and I love you." Everything went in complete silence and it was that type of silence where she thought he could hear her take a deep swallow. Drea was making steps towards her and she knew Drea was probably going to hug her and give her a kiss on her cheeks or forehead but this time he picked her up and spun her around. After spinning her around in his arms twice he lowered her down safely. She had felt like she had been wrapped in a warm blanket on a cold winter day. Drea asked her standing close to her did she know what a french kiss was she said yes and went right into telling Drea that she had never french kiss before. He said he knew that already and he was elated that she had not. They both starring each other directly in the eyes Shun'boo got on her tip toes and placed her arms around Drea neck and tilt her head slightly to the right and closed her eyes and there in that moment she experience her first french kiss.

It exceeded everything that she had imagine it would be. She had not thought well thoughts about her first kiss but Drea had kissed her causing everything in her world that was going wrong to have left that in another place. Her thoughts were being consumed in the present and there she was in the presence of the kiss which came to a perfect ending. Drea reaching and grapping both of her hands and placing it close to his heart. Only one thing she could say was she had a great day. Drea and Shun'boo had talked to her mom about her working and she agreed that she could work a little. She didn't know that Drea was working there. He had told them both while sitting talking with Shun'boo and her mom. After they had finish talking with her mom Drea and her chatted briefly about how she felt about working with him he said he was ok with it. Drea had said that it would be foolish to not want to see her as often as he could. They both laughed Shun'boo started working a week later. It was a lot to be able to perform especially for a young teenage girl. The job was not hard at all, but Shun'boo still had to do all her house hold chores that her mom wanted her to do and she didn't cut her any slack because she had started to work along with school as well. It was nice making earnest money. She would use majority of her money to buy her siblings and her the necessities they all needed. She would think how good it felt to be able to do so. Besides, she was glad not to ask Drea for money, even though Drea seems to never mine. He would just offer to help majority of the time.

However, things began to continue to go well with Drea and Shun'boo, but it seems money became another downfall. At least to her, Shun'boo mom's greed had taken her mom heart. She had placed so many demands on her daughter until she was barely able to perform and excel in school. She would be in class thinking about the demands she had on her and at the same time trying to hide as much as she could from Drea. She knew that he knew more than he probably should. He was a peacemaker. He would talk to Shun'boo about forgiveness a lot, and love. He would often tell her a lot of things will come and go even people, but he told

CHAPTER 10

Shun'boo next to the oldest sister had put on a pair of her tennis shoes without asking her. They were brand new shoes and expensive. Shun'boo never mind sharing with her sister, but she always ask them to ask her before getting anything. Her sister had worn the shoes without permission. When Shun'boo saw her sister with the shoes on, she ask her why did she not ask her to wear them and her sister said she did not have to ask to wear the shoes. It took Shun'boo by surprise that her sister had said that to her because they were close. She asked her sister could she take the shoes off because she did not ask and besides she had a negative attitude. Her sister told her that she was not taking the shoes off and the only way they were coming off her feet if Shun'boo had to remove them off her feet. She knew that meant a confrontation "fight." Shun'boo was never afraid of battling or "fighting." Where she was from she was a very strong and quick young girl. She never ever thought she would ever face her sister or any of her siblings for that matter in a battle. Shun'boo told her sister to take the shoes off again because she did not want it to lead to a fight. She also told her sister she didn't mind sharing anything with them, but she never have anything for herself. Shun'boo stated, that she is always giving and sharing everything with them. The things she purchase as well as the things that her mom and stepfather purchase for them occasionally. Even the things Drea had purchased her sister temperament escalated very quickly. Shun'boo had seen her sister get angry in this state with other people but not with her.

Shun'boo told her sister that she was going to let their mom know what was going on and as she was existing the bedroom her sister was standing in the way. Shun'boo asked her sister to move out of the way and her sister responded back and said make me and then she pushed her. Shun'boo response back was punches thrown within a few seconds. She had realized her sister was bleeding. Shun'boo went into shock and their mother heard the confrontation and their other siblings yelling stop! Her mother came in the bedroom asking what happened and seeing Shun'boo's sister bleeding from her nose. Shun'boo began crying, telling her sister that she was so sorry and their mother was yelling and blaming Shun'boo for everything. When she did not ask them both what had happened and how did it escalate into a fight, she told Shun'boo she was going to get punish for what she had done. The only thing she could think of at that time was how she had let herself come to such anger to ever fight her sister nevertheless fight any of her siblings. She loved them dearly and would never harm them. She was protective of them all as a young girl. Her mom told her sister to go and wash her face and she did. Shun'boo sat on the edge of the bed with so much hurt in her heart with the tears falling onto her lap with her head down. Her mother began telling her what her punishment was. She could hear her mom's voice speaking, but at the same time it was though she was not present. It was though her mother was speaking from a far distance.

Later that night as her sister and the other sister's lay in the full sized bed, her sister and her ended up laying by each other that night. She told her sister that she was truly sorry for what had happen earlier that day. Her sister and her hugged. It was one of the best hugs that Shun'boo had felt in a long time. At least, to her shattered heart that night, as she rolled over and vowed she promised to never let herself come to such angry ever again and never get mad enough to physically fight her siblings. Somewhere during the yelling, arguing, and fighting Shun'boo mother had ask Drea to leave. Shun'boo wondered what Drea was thinking. She was back and forth in her thoughts thinking did he think she was this horrible person, or the girl of genuine love for all people who he came to know. She just wanted to fall asleep. Morning came and it was a new day. It was Sunday! They did not attend church ever with her mother or step-father. God's name was never mentioned in their home as a child, but she could always feel this great protection with her that she couldn't explain what it was. The same presence that would be with her when she would have those horrible dreams of her fallen into a dark place and this presence would catch her every time during the fall. She always thought about a place of peace. She would use her imagination to go to that place of peace. As time went by, day by day the same as usual, the same family routine were followed. Shun'boo heart was becoming resentful to men even her love for Drea. The more abuse she saw that her stepfather had done to her mother the more her heart resented the human man.

She began to push Drea away. It was a warm weekend night which Drea had come back over and Shun'boo's mother had talked to her about having sex with Drea. Shun'boo's mom explained to her that he was not going to keep coming around and doing the things for her if she did not eventually have sex with him. She had harden her heart, but thought about her siblings and how they would be cared for. However, that same night she decided to give her virginity to Drea. She asked Drea to sit in the den and wait for her. She thought carefully how she

CHAPTER 11

She could see the desires in his eyes. She led Drea to the vacant apartment. He asked her what she was doing and she said nothing, but went straight into touching and kissing. Drea slow and passionate laid her down on the floor in the apartment and asked her did she really want to give her virginity to him. She could see in Drea eyes that he didn't really want to. He told her as he was over her that he never imagine himself loving her in a vacant apartment and that they could wait. He also told her it was no pressure. He just loved her. Drea pulled away from her. She took her hands and began touching Drea on his most male masculine body part and kissing him at the same time altering from his lips to his neck until he no longer could resist her and that he desired to go into her. As she helped guide his clothes off he gently as he could went into her. She gripped Drea back with her nails imbedded in his back with a slight pitch voice sound. She had outburst with Drea first stroke and a tear fell from her eyes of a broken spirit after a few minutes which seemed to her like it was hours. He asked her was she ok? He then kissed her forehead and told her that he would never leave her and he pulled out of her. He laid beside her trying to hold her, but she didn't want to be held. She was thinking about getting back to the apartment because she was having vaginal pain and she wanted to be by herself without any distractions so she could be alone with her thoughts. Drea got up to put his clothes on.

She didn't have to put her clothes on, only her panties because she had worn a sundress. He asked her as she was rushing him did she want to talk about what had just happened and if she was going to tell anyone what had happened. She told him no and who would care. By the look in Drea's eyes she knew in her heart that Drea cared. It was the same look he always had when he was around her and she knew Drea cared for her whole family. As Drea opened the door and paused he said, "Wait I love you." As they walked back to the apartment Shun'boo was thinking how she would enter the apartment knowing she had to see her mom. As Drea was about to enter the apartment with her she told him that she didn't want him to come in with her and asked him did he want to use the phone to call a cab. He said, "Yes." After Drea had placed the call he told her that he would wait outside until cab arrived. Drea hugged and kissed Shun'boo forehead and said good night. She headed up stairs to examine herself. She went into the bathroom to remove her panties and discovered she was bleeding. She was in pain. She took some tissue and placed it inside her panties and went and got her mother and asked her could she come in the bathroom. She told her mother that she had given her virginity to Drea and that she was having private pain. However, that's how her mom addressed her daughter's female feminine parts. She also told her mom that she was bleeding. Her mom told her to take a bath and that the pain that she was having was natural and it should go away soon.

She ask where was Drea and she told her mother he had left. She knew her mother would start questioning her about why he left. Before her mother could even ask, she told her that she had asked Drea to leave and that he had call a cab. Her mother said ok and left the bathroom. Shun'boo sat in the bathtub leaning back while feeling all the feelings of what her body was going through from the side effects of first time sexual intercourse and the emotional side of it as well. She finish taking a bath and cleaning herself up. She went into the bedroom where she slept and laid in the bed and into her thoughts she went into what had happen and how she couldn't change what had happen between Drea and her. She thought about Drea and how she felt unloved and uncared for by her mother. She thought how her mother showed little concern for her. Shun'boo laid their muffling her tears like great water drops falling from her eyes onto her pillow. She just wanted to sleep from that day forth. She knew in her very being it would change her during the middle of the week. At school she would find herself not being able to focus and the teacher took slight notice. Her teacher would catch her staring off. The teacher had called her out of the classroom into the hallway and asked her was she ok and she told her teacher yes everything was ok she was a wise young girl to not to arise any concerns with her. She told the teacher that she was on her period and sometimes it's hard to concentrate when she is menstruating. Her teacher said she do understand but focus as much as possible so she wouldn't miss important lecture that she would need when it was time to take tests.

Shun'boo said, "ok." Drea started staying some days at the restaurant just to see her. When she got to work she would be exhausted but would try to never show it. She was always thinking of her siblings and being able to help take care of them. Besides, she thought it allowed her time from the house where she lived. Most days Drea would give her money for a cab and sometime her mom would come and get her if her stepfather would let her mom get the car to come and get her. That happened only if Drea forgot to give her cab money or she forgot to mention it to

CHAPTER 12

Shun'boo and her siblings get an unexpected notice from their mom that they were going to move. She was glad for this move because where they were currently living was not so pleasant. Shun'boo had a couple of envy haters they had seen her with Drea and a few of them knew of Drea and liked him. In the area where they lived was full of drug pushers and people who were illegal drug users and all the drug pushers tried to get acquainted with her. She never gave them any interest. She had even gotten into two fights while living there. She also thought about the location. She was hoping it was a better living environment than where they were currently living. Shortly, within two weeks they had moved and Drea had help them moved. They had moved into a house which was better than an apartment. They had settled into the house within one week between her and her siblings, her mom, and stepfather and Drea's help. It was more than enough help to get settled fast. It appeared that her siblings enjoyed living in the house versus the apartment. Shun'boo always like seeing her siblings smile and laugh. Drea still would tell them some jokes even though Drea would always be the perfect gentleman. Shun'boo was a young teen girl whose spirit was broken. She started paying less interest to Drea as she did before. She thought that living in a different location would be better somehow even for the emotional side of her but things had gotten even worse. Her mom would make comments to her about her thinking that she was grown and since she had sex that she was "smelling herself," which meant in her house fast or smelling her female sexual aroused scent. That's how it was defined in her house.

It was one day while over the house Shun'boo step father saw Drea sitting in the den he said to Drea that he had notice that Drea always walked or took a cab where he was going. He had asked him did he know how to drive. Drea said, "Yes," but he needed more driving practice. Shun'boo thought what does he want because he didn't talk a lot to Drea which, Shun'boo didn't care if he did or if he didn't. He told Drea that on the weekends he could take him so he could get more driving practice. The following weekend he had taken Drea driving Shun'boo, her siblings and her mother were sitting in the den when they heard a loud crash, which sounded like it was in their den. Everyone was startled. They got up and went to look out the window and Drea had ran into the side of the house running the car into the pole which stood as the support of the carport. Everyone had gone outside to make sure they both were physically alright. They both where standing on the outside of the car and they both said they were alright and they both appeared to be ok. Drea said that he was truly sorry repeatedly. He said he didn't see the pole because it was dark. Shun'boo's stepfather told Drea it was ok. Everyone came in the house. Shun'boo's mom told Drea that he could sleep over because she would feel better if he did and make sure he was ok. Shun'boo was happy about Drea being able to spend the night. She went to the hallway linen closet and got Drea a sheet, blanket, and a pillow. Her siblings and her made the bed and changed the pillowcase on the pillow for Drea.

Shun'boo's mother attitude and mood quickly changed when she had come out of her bedroom from with her stepfather. Shun'boo already knowing why her mother mood changed because it was the weekend and her stepfather was going out and indulge himself with other woman, which was nothing new. The behavior from her stepfather has being going on for years along with all the physical abuse as well. Drea had not been at the house when the physical abuse would occur. Shun'boo would think she never wanted him to be around if they got into a physical fight because she didn't want to put Drea in the middle of anything. Shun'boo's stepfather had come into the den where Drea and her were sitting and asked Drea could he wear Drea's necklace. He told her stepfather, "yes," that he could where the necklace followed by, "can I have it?" Then Drea just smile and said sure if you really like the necklace. He took the necklace off and gave it to Shun'boo's step father. Her stepfather holding and examining the necklace in his hand then said to Drea this is a really a nice necklace and it has some weight too it. Drea said, "Yes." Shun'boo's step father said, "I will give it back to you Drea." Her stepfather left the kitchen. Drea looked at her and asked her was she tired and she said, "yes" and she wanted to take a hot bath and lay down. Drea asked was she hungry because he was and that he was going to order some pizza. She said she was not that hungry and that he could order pizza. He said, "Ok" and she told him that she would be back after she got a bath. Drea told her ok. Shun'boo went into the bedroom and got her clothes to wear to bed.

She went into the bathroom to run her bath water. She always hated when she had to go use the bathroom or to take a bath because it was two ways that you could enter into the bathroom. However, in her house going in either direction you had to past by her stepfather and mom's bed room. She just tried to avoid having to run into them and they

CHAPTER 13

He said, "ok." Before Shun'boo was about to turn and walk away Drea told her she looked so pretty as always and they both smiled. She left to go and clean the bathroom. While in the bathroom she could hear her stepfather and mom conversation. Her mom letting him know how she knew he was going to be with those whores and she could hear him say he did not know what she was talking about. She thought to herself hoping they don't start an argument that would lead into a fight and especially while Drea was at the house. She was done cleaning the bathroom when she heard the front door close. She knew it was her stepfather because he was the only who would use the front door if he was leaving to go out for the weekend. Furthermore, her siblings and her wouldn't see him go and commit God knows what, but they knew he indulged in something. Shun'boo knew her mom didn't leave out the front door. Her mom only went to the front door when someone rang the doorbell and she would sometime answer it always first looking out the window. Most of the time she would let Shun'boo answer it if she thought it was a business person looking for her or if she thought it was a bill collector coming to collect payment. Shun'boo would have to speak with them and tell them her stepfather and mom was not at home she hated being put in that position. Shun'boo went back into the den and dining area to make sure Drea and her siblings cleaned up the kitchen. They had finished cleaning and her siblings were in the room preparing for bed while Drea made a pallet on the floor. She told Drea that he could get a shower and he said ok.

She said he had to wait until her siblings finish getting their bath and they should be done in thirty minutes. He said, "Ok." She told him she would be back out to let him know when the bathroom was clean again. He said, "Ok." Shun'boo went in the bedroom and laid across the bed while her siblings where taking their bath. Her mom came in the bedroom to check and see what they all were doing. She asked did the den and dining area get cleaned. Shun'boo responded, "Yes" knowing her mom would still go and inspect the area. Shun'boo already knowing her mom she checked to make sure Drea and her siblings had cleaned the area. She said for them to make sure that the bathroom was cleaned. Her mom left the bedroom and Shun'boo could hear her mom asking Drea how he was feeling. He said he was ok. She was asking him because of the accident earlier in the car. He told her he was ok and that he was not hurting anywhere she said ok knowing that she was checking the area to see was it clean. To her satisfaction it must passed this time because there was no yelling after Shun'boo's siblings finished getting their bath and cleaned the bathroom. She had gotten a bath rag and towel for Drea and told him that he could get his bath and he said ok. Drea said, "You can go head and go to sleep", he told her that he would clean the bathroom and make sure the doors were locked. He cut off the lights and she said, "ok don't forget to cut the light off over the stove as well", he said, "Ok." She walked up towards Drea knowing he was not going to let her leave his presence without giving her a kiss.

He took his hands and placed them in her hands and leaned close to her and gave her a forehead kiss and told her goodnight. She gently pulled away from him smiled at him and said goodnight, thinking to herself how handsome and fine he was. He always made her feel like she mattered to him. Off to bed, Shun'boo went laying in the bed with her other three siblings her youngest sister. Her brother slept in the other room while her youngest baby brother slept with her stepfather and mother. As she laid there in the bed she always looked at her siblings and made sure the cover was evenly placed on them all. She laid there in the bed thinking how she didn't want Drea to think that she showed little compassion for him, by not asking if he was ok and if he thought she was being inconsiderate. Nevertheless, she stayed up until he finish showering and cleaning up. When Shun'boo opened her eyes it was a new day. She enjoyed hearing the birds chirping as though they were singing songs of praise of a new day. She looked around at her sisters to see if they were still sleeping and she would often call their names individually to see if they were awake. She called all their names and her second to the oldest sister said, "Yes" she was up just lying still resting. She got up and went to check on her siblings in the adjacent room. They were still sleeping. She didn't have to call their names because both of them where snoring loud. She smiled at them and went in the den where Drea was. He was awake already with the blankets folded up sitting on the couch with a cup in his hand drinking soda. Shun'boo did not like him drinking sodas all the time.

She would often let Drea know that sodas were not good too drink as often as he did. He smiled at her with that gorgeous smile that would make any person want to be around him. Even in his smile it was a feeling of pleasure. In his eyes, staring at Shun'boo, in a deep voice he gently said, "Good morning beautiful." She said, "Good morning

CHAPTER 14

He never really appeared to care about hurting neither her mom nor how Shun'boo heart would break. However, she would see the hurt in her mom eyes and even the sadness in the tone of her voice. Drea ask her was it some breakfast food to cook. She said to Drea you could have checked to see if there was food to cook since you took the courage to go open the refrigerator and pour yourself something to drink. He said, "Ok Miss Lady with your smart mouth," which Shun'boo had her way at times with her feisty mouth. She said, "Yes it was some breakfast food." She told Drea that she was going to brush her teeth and as she was leaving the kitchen. Drea said let me use your tooth brush. She said, "No" while laughing, then she said, "Yes," but he had to buy her another toothbrush. He said, "Ok." She left the kitchen, brushed her teeth, cleaned up a bit, and checked on her siblings. They all were awake except her siblings that slept in the adjacent room. She told them that Drea and her were going to cook breakfast and they smiled and ask was Drea still there. She said, "Yes." Her siblings enjoyed his company. She then went and knocked on her stepfather and mothers' bedroom door to let them know that she and Drea were going to cook breakfast. Shun'boo and Drea wanted to know if it was ok with her mom if they cook. Her mom said ok, but the sound of madness was in the tone of her voice. It was nothing for Shun'boo to hear her mom upset. She headed back into the kitchen with the toothbrush in her hand. She gave it to Drea and told him that he could go and brush his teeth. He said, "Ok."

She told him that she would start on breakfast. He said, "Ok don't half cook the food or burn it." She said, to Drea "ok, if I do I will be sure to give you the first plate with burned food." He laughed and left the kitchen. She began cooking breakfast. She decided to cook sausage, bacon, scrambled eggs, grits and toast. She thought to herself should she put the bacon back in the refrigerator because they were only allowed to have one breakfast meat. She also thought should she put the bread away as well because she thought that they could use it for sandwiches for lunch. Shun'boo thought that her mom would fuss at her about cooking all that food at one time since they were on a tight budget. She also thought that it should be ok since she was working part-time and she knew Drea would buy food for their house if they needed it. He had even bought new home decoration for Shun'boo's mom when she moved into the house. He was so thoughtful. Drea came back in the kitchen and told her that he had left the tooth brush in the bathroom. She said, "Ok" and he started to help cook breakfast. It was a lot to cook because they were cooking for eight people not including Drea and her. He was a great cook. Drea cooked at the restaurant and he enjoyed cooking especially making cornbread. He made the type of cornbread that should be tasted by all humanity at least once. It was that good and he knew he could cook some southern cornbread and he was swift when he cooked. She would glance up at Drea as they were cooking and he was smiling as she had seen him do before. He always had enjoyment on his face. He always seem to enjoy everything he did.

Shun'boo was so happy that Drea was helping cook breakfast for her siblings he had even said too her how he knew how she loved her siblings dearly and her mom. Drea had told her that day that he loved them all and that he always wanted her to love them no matter what happened. She thought there he go again trying to be a daddy to her and she didn't need that. He told her to not always think and analyze everything so much. It was though he could read her mind while smiling at her. By that time her sisters were coming in the kitchen and asking them was breakfast ready. Drea said that they just finished it while smiling at them. He said good morning to them and he told them he liked their hair styles. He had mentioned to Shun'boo that he had been asked to work in a hair salon under an apprentice. Shun'boo told her next to the oldest sister to go get her other siblings and Drea had her other siblings to sit at the dining room table as he brought their food. He did everything as he was a chef like the ones seen on television. He even had the kitchen towel tucked in over his belt. She thought again he was one fine man with all his fixtures manly and masculine. They all were in the kitchen and Drea asked her where was the extra folding chairs that they had used before. Shun'boo said, "On the back porch". He said, "Great." He would go quickly and get them. He came back and they all had seats. Even though it was not enough room at the table for them to place their plates on the table Drea and Shun'boo would just pull their chairs up to the table and place their plates in their lap and eat that way.

Drea asked her to go let her stepfather and mom know that breakfast was done. She went to let them both know that breakfast was done. They said, "Ok." While sitting at the table with them Drea told them that he liked their hair styles again and one of Shun'boo's sister told Drea that she did not like her hair. He asked her why did she not like her hair style. She said she didn't like a jerry curl. Drea said that she was still

CHAPTER 15

After she get the jerry curl unprocessed out her hair she explained to her mom that Drea said, he would pay for her hair to get treated at the hair salon. Drea said that he would pay for them to treat her hair after she got the jerry curl unprocessed out of her hair. Shun'boo's mom, asked Drea did he say that and he said, "Yes mama." She told her that since Drea was paying for it that she could get her jerry curl unprocessed out her hair. Shun'boo's sister was happy. She got up from the table and hugged Drea and said, "thank you." He said you don't have to say thank you but you are welcome. He told Shun'boo's other siblings that he would treat them all out to eat. They all were happy. The house phone had rang and Shun'boo's stepfather had answered the phone and come out into the dining area to tell Drea he had a call on the telephone. It was Drea's mother on the phone. He didn't look nervous at all but, Shun'boo was wanting to know why Drea mother was calling the house. The last time she called she was yelling at Drea asking him did he move his brother's clothing from the laundry room. Drea said, "thank you" to Shun'boo's step father and answered the phone. Her siblings got up from the table and started to clean up. Drea walked toward the den area and she could hear Drea saying that he was ok and that he would see her shortly. He said ok and hang up the phone. After Drea had gotten off the phone he told Shun'boo that his mom had called to check on him. Drea's mom had not seen or heard from him and that was not like him.

He said that he wanted to help them get everything clean up so he could go and see his mother before he went home. Shun'boo told Drea that he could leave because her siblings and herself would clean everything up and besides they had to do other chores. He said ok knowing that he wanted to go see his mom and then go home to get a shower and rest a little bit before he had to go back to work the following day. Drea called a cab the cab arrived in about twenty five minutes. Drea asked Shun'boo to walk him out the door. They both went out the side door. Drea kissed her gently on her lips and held her so gently close in his arms. She always had to stand on her tip toes when she hugged him. In his arms she felt safe. He said to her that he loved her and he would call her later once he got settle in at home. They both smiled as he left in the cab. When Shun'boo had come back in the house she started helping her sisters clean the house and their mom had come out her bedroom and ask was Drea gone and Shun'boo said, "yes." She thought how she wanted to finish cleaning up so she could get a hot bath and read the bible. Her mom never took them to church but Shun'boo had gotten a bible from church when she went with her grandmother. She kept it with all her special personal belongings. She would read it even though she didn't understand it at times. Her siblings and her finish cleaning everything up and even washed the dirty clothes and linens. They heard yelling coming from the bed room and they knew it was more than likely about Shun'boo's stepfather going out every weekend.

Then they heard bumping and yelling from their mom telling their stepfather to get off her and they could hear their baby brother crying. They all ran to their mom's bedroom. Shun'boo opened the door and her stepfather was beating her mom. She got her baby brother off the bed and handed him to one of her siblings to take him in another room where he would be safe. He would be safe in another room and they already knew to stay with him. Whomever she gave him to and the other two siblings would stay in the room as well. Shun'boo was a protector of her siblings and her mother. She began pulling her stepfather off her mom. As she was pulling him off her mom he would go in more rage because her mom would be trying to defend herself. He would began to hit her even harder. Shun'boo was very strong for her age and for her to be a teenage girl she would began to fight her stepfather. She could hear her siblings crying, and yelling for him to stop. He only stopped when he got tired and Shun'boo was not easily tired about anything especially if it had to do with her siblings. Shun'boo would get her mom safely from her stepfather however she had too. She even had knocked her stepfather out before by hitting him across his head with a VCR player because he had beaten their mom that time so bad. He had choked her until he was cutting off her airwaves. Shun'boo was so tired of all the abuse that was happening in her home knowing after her mom and settled down for a couple of hours away from her stepfather she was not going to leave him. It was though her life revolved completely around him.

He would leave most of the time and come back a couple of hours later. Her siblings and her would help their mom clean up the room when they had gotten in a fight and he had left the house. It was times he didn't leave and they both would clean it up together. If he left the house he would come into the den area where her mom was laying late in the midnight and ask her to come back in their bedroom and she would go. She could hear the sexual activity taking place because her mom would be loud. Shun'boo would be so nauseated with an upset stomach while

CHAPTER 16

Her mom started yelling at her telling her that she thought she was grown. Shun'boo mom would call her to her stepfather and mom bedroom and tell her to pour her stepfather and her something to drink. Shun'boo would be so mad that her mom would call her as though to punish her for her own tolerated unhappiness from her stepfather. No she was not happy about pouring him something to drink she would constantly call her as though she was being punished for helping protect her mom and he was mad because he thought she was being grown. He always said to her to stay in a child's place. Her mom always telling them too never call the police because she would go to jail as well. She would try to place fear in her siblings that she could get in trouble as well. Her mom would do anything to protect her stepfather out of her own fears but Shun'boo being young and wise her mom knew she could not tell her those lies. She knew they were all lies. Shun'boo didn't respect him as a man. She would think how he would beat her and leave bruises on her until she had to stay out of school. Shun'boo siblings would lay in the bed with her and cry. They would have to get ice to help heal the deep bruises which lasted for days. The bruises would sting when she tried to bath. It was hell leaving there it was never any rest for Shun'boo mind and body. However, at least she thought she was happier when

Drea was around. He brought comfort and even help buy some of her siblings and her necessities they needed.

Even though Shun'boo would think about the age difference between them Shun'boo had begun to have less trust for a man because of all she had seen and the things that were being implemented upon her. Also, the responsibilities of helping provide like an adult to help take care of her siblings. She would often think how they referred to her as always wanting to be grown. She thought how they had never took the time and thought how they both in their own way's caused her to grow up fast showing her what a grown unhealthy adult life looked like. She was filled with abuse and missing her childhood life. She never knew what that was and time would not let her have that back. Shun'boo, a young teenaged girl who spirit was broken by her stepfather and mother she would think I am not my mother's child where is her love and care for me. Shun'boo' loved her mom unconditionally. She knew it was going to be a long week. She thought how glad that spring break was coming. Soon they would be out of school for summer break. Monday's were always the hardest day for her siblings to adjust too. They were more sluggish and lest active after spending seven hours at school. Shun'boo just wanted to go home straight from school. She was exhausted from the past weekend, but she had to be at work at 4:30 p.m. When she got there she would normally see Drea. He would be in the dining area of the restaurant waiting for her to arrive. She let the owner know that she had arrived and she went to the back to look for Drea. He was not in the kitchen area. She heard a bumping sound which sounded like it was coming from the outside.

She went out to see if Drea was out in the food storage room. When she opened the door she found Drea in the storage area. He turned around and smiled and said, "Hey beautiful." She said, "Well good afternoon." He appeared busy. He was pulling food from the freezer to take into the restaurant for the next day's menu. She asked Drea would he like some help. He said that he was ok, but thanked her for asking if he needed help. He told her that she was thoughtful. She smiled and said, "Ok" as she mentioned she was going back into the restaurant too get to work. Shun'boo went in and began serving. A lady ask her was Drea there and she said, "Yes." She started to wonder what the lady wanted with Drea. She asked could Shun'boo go get Drea after she finish paying for her food. After she paid for her food, Shun'boo ask Fredrick could he go get Drea because someone wanted him. He said, "Sure." She appeared to be a little older than Drea possibly in her mid-twenties. Shun'boo observed that the young lady was looking at her while she was waiting on Drea to come out. Drea came from the back and Drea ask Shun'boo who was out there to see him. She told Drea that the young lady who was sitting at one of the corner tables. Drea appeared to have known the young lady. He went out to the dining area and sat down at the table with her. Shun'boo thought if Drea was seeing that young lady behind her back she said he would not get away with it. She continued to work while glancing over at them both. The young lady and Drea went outside. They went out the front door of the restaurant.

If they would had left and gone out the side door of the restaurant they would have to pass by Shun'boo. Shun'boo thought to herself. Did Drea intentionally go out the front door to avoid having to pass by her? Shun'boo stood looking outside through the large windows of the restaurants. She was looking to see if Drea and the young lady would show any kind of affection towards each other. The young lady hug Drea and Drea hugged her, but it was not the same hug. Everyone was watching to see how Drea would hug her. Everyone that was in

CHAPTER 17

Even though her mom was aware of this behavior Shun'boo never could be comfortable around this kind of behavior. Matty came out and ask were they finish cleaning up the restaurant. She would help out if they were behind. After she finish counting the money she told the owner of the restaurant that they were done. Drea had not arrived yet. She knew that he would not stand her up. At least she knew he would call her if anything changed and he could not pick her up. He came finally. Matty asked her was she going to call a cab and she told her that Drea was coming to pick her up. She noticed that a car was pulling in on the property of the restaurant and she told Matty that it had to be Drea. Shun'boo walked closer to the window to see was that Drea and it was him all cleaned up and handsome as usual. He came into the restaurant smiling as usual. His teeth were pearl white as though he just came from the dentist getting them cleaned. His clothes perfectly pressed, and hands always manicured. He also had round brown eyes with long eyelashes. He was gorgeous and a sight to see. The smell of his cologne mix so well with his body chemistry. He spoke to everyone and they all complimented him on how nice he looked. Drea was always polite and said, "thank you." Fredrick ask where they going on a date. Shun'boo answered the question before Drea could say anything and said, "NO."

Drea smiled and said that can change. Then Matty told them goodnight and to be safe as they left. As Drea was pulling out of the restaurant parking lot Shun'boo told Drea that she wanted to go straight home. He said to her that he wanted her to come over to his house.

She said to him that she had to call her mom while thinking how she didn't want to get out of the car to use a payphone. He told her that he had already called her mom and she said that it was ok for her to come over his house. Her mom told Drea that she had to be home by 9:45. When Drea and her pulled up to the house before getting out of the car he told her that he loved her. Shun'boo didn't say anything. She opened the door and got out while grabbing her book bag, purse, and a plate of food she had purchased from the restaurant. Shun'boo was trying to carry everything because she didn't want Drae to help her with anything. It was her way of letting him know that she could help herself without him. He came around on the side of the car grabbing for her things that were in her hand. She said to him that she had it. He said, "Are you sure?" She replied, "Yes, I'm sure" in a smart tone of voice. He took his hand and rubbed it down her face laughing at the same time saying you are feisty. He told her to watch her step as she entered onto the front porch. When they got inside, Drea roommate Lonnie was in the living room watching television and talking on the phone. He removed the phone from his ear and said, "Hey Shun'boo, How are you? Glad to see you!" He told her that it has been a while since he seen her and he told her she looked nice. She said, "thank you." As Drea said, jokingly to Lonnie to keep his eyes off her they all laughed. He said to her, if I don't see you before you leave take care.

She said, to him "thank you and likewise." Drea took her by her free hand and walked her to his bedroom. She sat her things down in Drea's room and asked him could she use the bathroom. He said, "Ok I will walk you across the hallway and wait outside of bathroom until you come out." She said, I'm not a toddler and I can use the bathroom by myself." He said, to her that he was sure of that but, he was not taking no for an answer. He said, besides this is an all-male living quarters. She said, "Ok drill sergeant." After coming out the rest room Drea was standing outside like he said. Shun'boo sat on his bed. Not only did Drea take care of his self, but his room was clean also. He asked her did she want something to drink. She said, "I hope it is water because I don't drink sodas like you do." He said, "I know that miss beautiful." He told her that he would be right back and he was closing the door for privacy and protection. She said, "For protection." He said, "Yes because if anyone of my roommates comes back here and see that the door is close they will knock first." She said, "Ok." Drea came back shortly, he handed her the glass of water. She told Drea "thank you" for the water, but she wanted to talk to him about who the young lady was that came to the restaurant to see him earlier that day. Drea sat next to her on the bed and told her that she was someone he used to date before her. He said that it was nothing between them. He told Shun'boo that he told the young lady that he was dating someone.

Drea said he had to be careful about letting just anybody know he was dating her because of the age difference. Shun'boo said, "alright but, if she come back looking for you at the restaurant he will have to let her know that he was dating her. He said, "Yes beautiful." She told him how nice and clean the room was and Drea told her that he took extra effort to make sure the room was clean because he knew that she was coming over. She said "Oh really! You did." He said this while they both were sitting close to each other. Drea pulled her close to him and began kissing her slow and passionate. He asked her was it ok for him to touch her? She said, "Yes." Drea was always gentle with her. He assured her with his well-chosen words that he would be gentle with her and he was. Shun'boo asked him to go to the bathroom with her. She asked could she just take a shower at his house so when she got home she would not have to worry about showering. He said, "Yes." Drea bath her and kept asking was she alright she told him she was alright trying not to show the discomfort she was feeling. After he had bathe her he helped her out the shower and dried her off and she got dress. This time she let Drea get her things. He even got her purse and carried it as well. She began smiling. He asked her what she was smiling at when they were getting into the car. She told him that she was observing his thoughtfulness and it made her smile. At the same time Shun'boo was thinking how it would be if her stepfather and mother gave thought to her like Drea.

Shun'boo wanted to be shown love by her stepfather and mother. He said it was a joy to see her smile. He told her that her smile was priceless. She didn't stay far from Drea. He pulled up to the house and she told him that she didn't want him to walk her to the door because she was fifteen minutes late arriving home. He told her that he would walk her in the house. Shun'boo rung the door bell and her stepfather opened the door. He spoke to Drea and went back to his room. He hugged her and gave her a kiss on her forehead and said goodnight. Shun'boo went straight to the bedroom where she shared a room with her sisters. They all were asleep except her sister that was next to the oldest. Shun'boo took off her clothes and changed into her night clothes. She was glad that she had taken a shower at Drea's house. She open the closet and put here things away and laid down. Shun'boo's sister ask her what did her and Drea do that night. She told her she would have to tell her on their way to school the following day because she was tired. She laid there thinking how she would have to wake an hour earlier to complete her homework. She told her sister goodnight and feel asleep. The week had went by fast. It was Friday and Shun'boo sister reminded her that she didn't tell her about what happened between her and Drea. She told her that Drea was a gentle caring guy. She believed that he cared for her, but she still had this wall of protection up because she had witness their stepfather lack of love and respect for their mom. She asked her did she give her virginity to Drea.

CHAPTER 18

She told her sister yes and not to ask her anymore questions. She said, "Ok I will agree to not ask you anymore question if you answer this last question." Shun'boo said sure you can ask me your last question. Her sister ask her was she planning on having sex with Drea again. Shun'boo said to her sister to answer your question she never intended to or even thought of giving her virginity to any guy not at the time that it happen. She said to her sister that the only things that consistently consumed her thoughts was love to be present in their stepfather and mother hearts for each other. Also, that love would be given and shown too her siblings and her in its purest form and too have peace. Shun'boo said to her sister that she was tired and she was going to sleep. It had been a while since Shun'boo had a dream that she would be walking on this path and unaware of this dark hole. She would fall into it as always and this strong hand, but gentle at the same time would grab her out of the hole safely. In the dream Shun'boo would be walking headed somewhere living life purposely but unaware or not expecting this dark hole would appear and not see that she would fall into a hole. Looking around for help, and without a spoken word help came. Shun'boo woke up sitting straight up in the bed. She looked around at her sibling seeing that they all were sleeping. She just said openly out loud but softly where she would not awaken them that "she love them all." She laid back down and closed her tired eyes. She felt the heaviness of them and drifted off to sleep. She was awaken by the birds chirping. It was always a pleasant sound to her ears.

Her siblings and her got up to start the day. While Shun'boo was getting dressed she heard her sister calling her name. She was the third born child. She asked her sister what did she want and she ask Shun'boo could she wear her tennis shoes. She ask her sister what tennis shoes. She said your newest Jordan's. She said I just got those. She told her sister that she could wear them but not to wear them out and make sure she take care of them. Shun'boo felt the need to tell her sister that because her sister was known for being lazy and not taking good care of things. Her sister told her 'Thank you," and she would put them back in the shoe box when she got home from school. Shun'boo said alright. She told her sister that the shoes looked perfect with her attire for the day and they both laughed knowing her sister was happy to wear her tennis shoes. Shun'boo told them that before they left out for school that she was going to give them all money to buy their snack at school and to buy them some sweet treats after school. Shun'boo and her next to the oldest sister attended the same school and their other brother and sisters attended the same school. Off to school they all went. When her sister and her got inside the school building Shun'boo told her that she had to use the restroom, and ask her if she could go and get her books she needed for class. Her sister said, "Ok." While in the restroom Shun'boo was approached by a girl who asked her did she know Drea? She told her "yes" she knew Drea, and she ask were Drea and her still dating each other.

She ask the girl why did she want to know. She told her that she was not an open book to a stranger. The girl laughed and said that she was not a stranger to Drea. She told Shun'boo that she had dated Drea before and she was currently talking back to Drea. Shun'boo told her that she just don't take what a stranger tells her as if it's the truth. Shun'boo finished washing her hands and checked her hair and makeup and left the restroom. Her sister was coming down the hallway and ask her was she alright. Shun'boo said, "Yes, and why did you ask was I alright." Her sister told her that by her facial expression she appeared as something had disturbed her. She said that she would tell her sister what had happened in the restroom. Her sister said, "Ok" and they would talk after school. While in class Shun'boo would think about what the girl had mentioned to her in the restroom and what had happened at the restaurant.

She knew she couldn't just disregard everything. As she sat in her first period class thinking what is done in the dark it will surface to the light. She knew this to be true because she had seen it repeatedly between her stepfather and mother even with her extended family's dark issues. She thought how darkness had to always face its greatest component "LIGHT." While changing classes throughout the day she would see her sister between their third and fourth period class. They would meet at the locker. She knew when her sister and her met at the locker that she would be watching her to see if it was something she should have a concern about. After all Shun'boo's siblings knew that she had a lot of haters and jealous girls.

CHAPTER 19

Even women at times were jealous. Shun'boo was a very beautiful girl. She was petite, but very well figured girl. She had a caramel skin tone with bright brown eyes. You would notice her eyes upon the sunbeam. You could see the hazel around the iris of her eyes, and her voice was pleasant. She was always well dressed and took well care of her body. She had a very distinctive walk. She was a head turner and beautiful to the eye. Most of the fights that her siblings and her had gotten into at their previous addresses were because of the jealously she encountered. All the guys were trying to get a date with her or even a telephone date....... lol.... She thought that they all were immature which was the truth. They all were boys who matured slower than girls in their own way as well as their behavior habits. Besides, she didn't have time to give energy to that. She had enough to face at home. She was not trying to add any drama to her life. Shun'boo sister reminded her at the locker that she wanted to know what happened in the restroom. She told her sister there was no reason to worry and that she would tell her what happened. Her sister said, "Alright" and they both went to class. Finally, it was the last class for the day. Shun'boo met her sister at the locker. They would normally put their books up if they had no homework to complete. They headed down the hall and out of the school building.

Before Shun'boo could ask her sister how her day was and her sister anxiously ask Shun'boo what happened. She told her while standing there waiting on the bus to come that after she had used the restroom she came out of the stall and a girl asked her did she know Drea.

She told her sister the girl also stated, she was still dating him. She told her that she don't give information to strangers or share her personal life with them neither. She thought it was not her exact words but they were somewhat close to them. Her sister ask her what happen after that. She told her that she washed her hands and checked her makeup and left the restroom. Her sister ask did she think, or did the girl give her any indication that she would be a problem. Shun'boo said, "What! A problem." She told her sister in a very firm and direct tone she didn't care to solve other people's problem whether it was personal or to be left alone especially if confusion was brought about and they try to involve you. She told her sister that if the girl came to her again and addresses her about Drea or anything that she would handle her accordingly. Shun'boo was no push over. Her sister said, "Alright" and that she hoped that the girl didn't say anything else to her about anything. Shun'boo's bus stop was coming up. She told her sister that she would see her later and to go straight home and to be safe. Her sister said, "ok" and she got off the bus to head to work. She only had a short distance to walk from where the bus stop was. Shun'boo was thinking as she was walking up to the restaurant how she didn't want to ask Drea about the girl who she saw at school that morning, and besides she didn't even know the girl name. The only thing she knew was they attended the same school. When she entered the restaurant Drea was waiting on her. He asked how her day was and gave her a hug. She told him that it was an interesting day.

Drea said, "How was it interesting?" She told him that she would tell him about it when she got off from work and that he could call her at home. He ask her was she alright. She said, "yes, and Drea ask her did she have money because if she needed money he would give it to her. She told him that she had enough money for the rest of the week. She reminded Drea that he said that he would get her sister hair done this coming weekend. He told her he was glad that she reminded him because it had slipped his mind with him being busy working at the restaurant, changing some things around at his house, and helping his mom. Drea smiled and said, "don't worry I got her." She said, "Ok" and put her book bag and her purse away. She used the restroom and went to work. Another day had went by and she was glad to be at home to take a hot bath. She always enjoyed that time alone. She was preparing for the next day by choosing what clothes to wear. She thought about how blessed she was because she could recall not so long ago she didn't have many clothes to choose from. Since meeting Drea and working she was fortunate to buy her some clothes. Drea had bought majority of her clothes. He was always happy to see her happy even though she was difficult to understand at times. Drea told her that he had a mom who raised him and he couldn't understand her, but he simply loved and respected her. He told her that if he never understood her completely that he loved her at his best. Shun'boo would think what Drea meant about loving her at his best. She never asked him what he meant.

Shun'boo was hoping Drea would call as she finish everything she needed to do, such as completing her homework. The house phone rang and it was Drea. He said, "What's up girl." The pitch and tone in his voice could make a girl's heart pitter patter. She said, "You are what is up." Drea laughing on the other end of the phone with excitement in his voice saying he always like to hear that. She said, "Ok Mr. Drea, but

Chapter 20

Then Drea said "yes," but please let me explain myself. She told him that he had lied to her and deceived her. She told him that it was over between them and hung up the telephone. The phone rang again. She knew it was Drea so not to disturb or alarm her mother she quietly put the ringer on silence. She made herself a mental note to cut the phone back on first thing in the morning. She was devastated at what Drea had just told her. So no one would hear her groans or see her crying she went into the laundry room which was located in the back of the house. No one could hear her in that area, besides the door in the laundry room had a lock. She fell to the floor on her knees and cried countless tears from the betrayal and lies of Drea. Drea was the one person other than her mother and siblings whom she loved dearly. Even though she didn't express it to Drea because of the seed her step-father had planted in her heart. All the selfishness acts her stepfather had done came to her thoughts. Now she had come to know that Drea betrayed her. Off her knees Shun'boo laid in the fetal position on the floor holding her stomach. It seem that from the depths of her belly she was giving birth to pain. After she couldn't cry anymore tears she told herself that she would make sure Drea knew how he hurt her that night. Shun'boo also told him that every relationship is a game. Besides family she gave no thought to a relationship with God because she didn't know of him. However, little did she know that he knew her very well!

He was her "Heavenly Father," that she would soon come to know, and he also kept close watch of every aspect of her life. She thought sharing with Drea her life, time, space, thoughts, and her love for him was all a game. She thought he played the game until he could know longer hide it. She took one of the towels that were folded from the linen closet which was located inside the laundry room and wiped her face. In the laundry without knowing she opened herself to inflict hurt and receive hurt from people. No one heard her because everyone was asleep. Furthermore, with little sleep Shun'boo woke up to the birds chirping. She loved to hear the sound of them as though they were singing songs of praise and thankfulness of a new day. The sound was beautiful but betrayal wouldn't let her heart rejoice to be alive and to hear them rejoice on a new day. She was always happy to see her sisters and brothers in the morning. She thought even if Drea was not going to be around or in their lives any longer that she would still take care of them. She was always checking to make sure they were alright. She would ask them before leaving out of the house for school if they all needed money for snacks. Her sisters that were in elementary school told her that they needed money to buy some things from the book fair. Shun'boo was happy to have money to give them to buy some things they wanted from the book fair. She remembered when she was in elementary and her stepfather and mom didn't have money to give them for the book fair.

Shun'boo went and got her savings account which she kept inside their bedroom closet in a white shoe box inside a white basket. She had notice that someone had been in it again and taken money out. She didn't like any of her sisters taking anything from her without asking. She never made a big fuss about them taking money from her. She would just talk to them and tell them that she knew someone was taking money and that it was called stealing which was not good behavior. Shun'boo told them that they all knew that they could come to her if they needed anything or just extra money to buy something. All of her siblings would listen to her most of the time. Shun'boo finish getting dress for school and as they were leaving out the door she remembered to turn the ringer on the telephone back on. While walking to the bus stop with her sister, she told her sister that she had been getting nauseous and that she was extremely nauseated at the present moment. Her sister said to her do you think you need to turn around and go back home. She thought how nice it would be to go home and lie down to rest. However, she knew her mom wouldn't just let her lie down and rest. Shun'boo thinking first her mom would accuse her of not being sick. She wouldn't be able to lay down shortly because she knew her mom would say that she could only lay down for a while. Her mom believed laying down only made you feel worst and a lot of times her mom appeared to not like her laying down. She recall her mom waking her up out of her sleep numerous of times to get up and clean up or fold clothes.

Even in the middle of the night Shun'boo thought she would rather go to school. There was no loving care for her at home and no restful place. She told her sister she would rather go to school. She was getting even more nauseous riding on the bus, such as motion sickness. She told her sister that she had to get off the bus and asked her sister to pull the cord for the bell to ring so they could get off immediately. Her sister pull the cord and the bust stopped and her sister began helping her up out of the seat and off the bus. Shun'boo noticed the bus driver looking at them through the inside mirror of the bus. He was looking at them with a curious look on his face. He knew that he was letting them off at an awkward spot and not their usual bus stop. He had gotten familiar with their faces because that was his regular bus route. Shun'boo stepped off the bus first with her sister behind her. She walked over to a grass area and began vomiting. Her sister patting her on her back and yelling "are you ok!" Shun'boo was unable to speak at the moment. Her sister said do you want to stay here while I try to find a pay phone nearby and call home to let mom know you are sick. She told her sister that she didn't want her to call home. She asked her sister could she get some napkins out of her purse so she could wipe her mouth. She also asked her sister to get a piece of gum out of her purse for her to chew on. Shun'boo told her sister they would have to walk the rest of the way to school.

Her sister asked her was she sure it would be ok and was she able to make it. Shun'boo told her sister she thought it would be ok and stated it is not that far. Her sister said that she would carry her book bag for her. She did not want her sister to carry her book bag for her because she was thinking the weight from her sister's book bag along with her own would tire her out. She dreaded having her sister carry both of their book bags. Shun'boo knew her body was weak and she knew she had to preserve her energy to walk the rest of the way to school. She told her sister that she would buy her something nice that she wanted for being thoughtful and for helping her. Shun'boo sister said to her that she didn't have to buy her anything because that's what sister's do. Sister's help each other, especially when in need. She said to her sister that's right, but I'm still buying you something. Her sister shook her head. Her sister said, as they arrive at school "you know we are late." She replied, "Yes, and I know we will be counted tardy today." They both headed to the office to check-in. Her sister asked, "What are we going to tell the school receptionist?" Shun'boo said the truth, which is me getting sick on the way to school. Her sister said, "Ok, but they still might call mom. Shun'boo thinking to herself that her sister was right because the school has a tendency to call the parents about everything. While her sister was signing in Shun'boo escape the office and started running to the restroom. She did not make it to the restroom in time and vomited on the floor. She heard her sister calling her name, "Shun'boo" her sister said, "Let me help you."

CHAPTER 21

She told her that the school was calling their mom to inform her that she was sick and that they arrived late because she had gotten sick on the way to school. She told her sister ok. As they were coming out of the restroom the school nurse came up to Shun'boo and asked her how she was feeling. Shun'boo said, "Alright." The school nurse had walked on the other side of her holding on to her arm to help give her more support. While walking her sister was holding her other arm. They took her in the nurse office and laid her on the nurse's bed. The school nurse told her sister that she could stay with her sister because their mom had told the school receptionist that she would be up to the school to check them both out. She told them that she would be right back she had to pull her school record folder to see if their mom had given the school permission for her to be cared for by the school nurse. Mrs. Stinson return back shortly and told them that their mom did not sign the permission slip giving her consent for the school nurse to administer medicine to her. The information that the nurse told them did not surprise Shun'boo because she knew her mom would not want her to be seen by the school nurse, especially when she had bruises on her from the beatings she would get. Even though a lot of the physical punishment had stopped and Shun'boo was getting older she was very defensive toward the harsh punishments. Shun'boo was not a problem child. She did things along the lines of what your typical teenage child would do. For example: She would sneak and eat cookies when she knew she wasn't supposed to be eating them, or put on makeup before it was time for her to start wearing it.

However, the things Shun'boo did were not reasons for such harsh punishment. Shun'boo would sometimes think that her mom thought that she would reach out for help when she would get beaten by them for no justifiable reason. Everything they had done to her mentally, emotionally, and physically was never justifiable. Her mom would apologize to Shun'boo. "YES THIS HAPPENS", only from fear of her telling someone what she was enduring. Her mom had arrived at the school to check them out. Shun'boo mom's countenance appeared that she was angry with them both. She didn't ask her how she was feeling or anything. She told them let's go after she signed them out. She told Shun'boo she knew she was sick before leaving the house that morning. Her mom told her that she was going to punish her for having to call her stepfather to pick her up from school. The only reason she called her step father was because she couldn't find another person to come get her. She told Shun'boo that this could have been avoided if she would have told her she was sick before leaving the house. That morning she knew her stepfather had already discussed with her mom that he was unpleased with her calling him. He was concerned about having to leave work. Her stepfather didn't like missing work for anything, which was one good quality she saw in him. Her mom asked her stepfather to drop her sister off at home first then she would take Shun'boo to the emergency room. Shun'boo mom thought she should be seen by a doctor. Shun'boo mom rarely took them to a primary care doctor only for shots when they were younger. They would go to the Health Department for a yearly physical. They had arrived to the house to drop her sister off.

Shun'boo mom told her sister to call Drea at his job to let him know that Shun'boo was sick and they were on the way to the hospital. Shun'boo asked her mom why you would have my sister to call Drea. Her mom told her that she should never question her about anything and whatever she say goes because she is her mother. Shun'boo had little energy. She just laid back with her head laying backwards. She closed her eyes thinking how she wanted to escape her present environment. Her stepfather told her mom that he was not going to the emergency room. He told her mom she could drive the car. Shun'boo stayed in the back seat while her mom drove her to the emergency room. Her mom told her that she had a very smart mouth and she better not try her again with those smart comments. They arrived at the hospital and Shun'boo mom mentioned to her that she needed to keep her mouth shut and not talk about anything that she shouldn't. Shun'boo knew exactly what her mother meant. Her mom was referring to anything that happened in their home. Her mom asked, "Did you hear me Miss Shun'boo?" Anytime her mom called any of her sisters "Miss' followed by their names she would be irate. Shun'boo said, "Yes mama" as they went inside. While sitting there to see the doctor Shun'boo told her mom that she had to go to the restroom because she felt like she was about to vomit again. Shun'boo went to the restroom and vomited. She then rinsed her mouth out and washed her hands before coming out. She came out of the bathroom hoping they would call her name. As soon as she got ready to sit down they called her name. They called her into the triage exam room.

CHAPTER 22

After they finished triaging her they walked her and her mom to a room. The nurse ask her when was her last menstrual period. She told them that she was about three days late, but it was normal for her because she would be late sometimes. The nurse gave her a gown to change into and a cup to collect a urine specimen. The nurse ask her if she was able to give a urine sample. She told the nurse, "yes." Shun'boo thought to herself saying "I'm glad that I didn't use the restroom earlier before they called me to the back." The nurse left the room and her mom told her that she better not be pregnant. She told her how hard her life would be if she was pregnant. She looked at her mom with so much disappointment. Shun'boo then left the room to find a restroom. She didn't see a restroom in sight and stopped to ask one of the nurses who was walking by. The nurse told her to follow her and said, "I will show you sweetheart." Shun'boo trying not to cry held in her tears because that was the first time she had someone other than her sister say or show her that they care. Shun'boo also told the nurse "Thank you," because she had helped her walk to her office earlier that day. The nurse told her she was welcome and she hoped she feel better while placing her hand on her back to comfort her. She went into the restroom to urinate collecting part of her urine in a cup, which was the clean catch part of the urine.

She washed her hands and looked in the mirror. Her face was pale and her eyes appeared glowless. Her lips were dry and cracking.

While standing in front of the sink two over-sized tear drops fell from her eyes onto the sink. She turned the water on to rinse her tears away which had fallen in the sink. She took a napkin to dry her face. Shun'boo felt as though God had come when she was at her weakest mind set or lowest point to wash away her tears and completely dry them up. Shun'boo left the restroom and return back to the room. Her mom told her when she came into the room that it took her forever to go and collect some urine. She heard a voice say, "Hey, how are you" and it was Drea. He had come while she was in the restroom. She was not excited to see Drea, but she said, "Hello Drea" in a formal way. Shun'boo began to get up on the bed. Drea ask her if she needed any help while gently grabbing her legs placing them comfortable on the bed. He reached for the blanket and covered her up. He leaned over and gave her a forehead kiss. However, this was the first time that Shun'boo mom had seen Drea give genuine care to her. Drea would often give her a head, back, and foot massages when she was exhausted. Shun'boo just wanted to know what was going on with her and she wanted to feel better. Her mom had told Drea that the doctor was going to do a pregnancy test on her and she had talked to Shun'boo earlier before he arrived. She explained to Drea that she told Shun'boo that she better not be pregnant. Shun'boo thought to herself that the doctor had not come into the room yet to examine her. The nurse also had not said anything to her mom yet nor mention the results of the pregnancy test.

Even though Shun'boo knew they would take a pregnancy test on her. Drea had said to her mom that he didn't want to say or do anything to hurt Shun'boo or make either of them mad at him. He told her mom

that if Shun'boo was pregnant that he would take care of her and the baby. Shun'boo told Drea and her mom that she knew that she was not pregnant. She hoped she wasn't because her stepfather would always say to her mom that she would probably end up pregnant. Shun'boo would enjoy going to the skating rink, and school dances with her aunt who was a couple of years older than her. Shun'boo had fun hanging out with her aunt which was a time that she gave no thought to what she was enduring. At her aunt house she felt free with the liberty of being a teenager. Her aunt would style her hair. Sometimes Shun'boo sisters would come by and they all would dress alike. Sometimes no one could rock that 'SALT AND PEPPER OR SPINDERALLA" look alike. Shun'boo was the only one to rock those styles.........lol..........
Her aunt didn't influence her in any negative way. Her aunt was always happy to see her and Shun'boo's sister enjoying themselves. Shun'boo didn't want the words of her step-father to come to pass at least this time she didn't. The doctor came in the room and introduced himself and before asking her mother and Shun'boo any questions he ask was it ok for Drea to stay in the room. Shun'boo ask Drea to step out of the room until the doctor finished examining her. He said, 'alright" and he would wait in the hallway outside her room. The doctor continued with his examination questions and physical exam. The doctor explained to her mom that they ran a series of test on Shun'boo.

The doctor also stated, he was going to have some blood drawn and the he would give her some medicine for nausea and vomiting along with an IV fluid. The IV fluid was to help her start feeling better, which sounded like pleasant music to Shun'boo's ears. Before the doctor left the room her mom ask the doctor would they do a pregnancy test on Shun'boo. He said, "Yes" and left the room. Her mom then step outside the room. Shun'boo was thinking her mom stepped out to let Drea know that is was ok for him to come back in the room. Drea came in and walked over to Shun'boo and said to her that everything was going to be alright. Shun'boo mom ask Drea could he stay in the room with her until she go and use the restroom and get something to drink. She also told Drea to come get her if the nurse or doctor come back to the room before she return and let them know where she was. Drea replied, "Alright" and he would let them know if they were to come in the room looking for her. It was the first time Drea and Shun'boo had been alone since seeing him at the restaurant and telling him what happened at the school concerning the girl who confronted her. The girl told her that she and Drea had started back talking and he would call her. Drea admitted to having sex with her. Shun'boo thought she was just a sexual partner or did Drea have feelings for her. Also, Shun'boo wondered were there other girls or young ladies he was sleeping with as well. She thought about the young lady who had come to the restaurant looking for him and he sat at the table with her in the dining area of the restaurant.

CHAPTER 23

Furthermore, nothing that Drea said would matter to her at this point. The pain in her heart which Drea had caused made her heart ache and wouldn't let her see him in a compassionate way. She could not see the compassion that she once had for him. The hurt she was feeling in her heart was about to manifest into deep hatred against the male race. Drea told her that he wanted to talk to her about something he was struggling with. He told her that it was not the time nor place to talk about the situation Shun'boo didn't say anything to Drea. He told her that whatever happened between them he love her and he always will. She felt compassion breakthrough for a moment and within that moment Drea and her eyes connected with a unity of love. When the moment had passed the love she felt for Drea had subsided to a place where there was no hurt nor was she angry. At last, she had a hold on her heart again and it was as though love couldn't come and then go away, but hate she thought could be present at any moment or not present at any moment. In the moment with Drea and her "Love was a powerful source." Shun'boo mom had return back to the room and ask had the nurse or doctor come back in the room. However, before they could answer there was a knock on the door. The door swung open and it was Shun'boo's nurse. She told her that she was about to draw her blood, start an IV, and give her some fluids. She would also be given her medicine as well. The nurse that was caring for Shun'boo, Drea ask her how long had she been a nurse.

She glanced up at Drea and said, 'I can't tell you that because you might figure out my age. They all laughed including her mom. She told them that she had been a nurse for a while and she truly enjoyed her job. The nurse stated, she love to take care of people. Drea told her that he could tell by her gentleness and care towards Shun'boo. She smiled with a warm smile and said, "Thank you." After the nurse had completed the orders the doctor gave her she told them that she would be sending the blood work and urine to the lab. She also told them that the test results shouldn't take too long to come back and that the doctor would be back in the room to talk to them once he receive the results. The nurse ask Shun'boo was there anything else she could do for her. Shun'boo said, "Yes, can you please bring me another warm blanket. The nurse said, "Sure sweetie," which was the second time Shun'boo heard a nurse address her in that manner. By Shun'boo hearing the word "sweetie" it was comfort to her because she was weak, tired, and sick. She told Shun'boo mom that it was a nurse call button on the side of Shun'boo bed that she could use if Shun'boo needed anything. Her mom said, "Thank you." She told them that she would be right back with blankets. Shun'boo mom asked Drea to turn on the television. She told Drea to put the television on her soap channel. Drea already knew what channel to put the television on because his mother watched soaps as well. There was a knock on the door and it was the nurse with the blankets. She unfolded the blanket and place the warm blanket on Shun'boo chilled body.

Shun'boo told the nurse "thank you" as she exited the room. Shun'boo and Drea's mom did a lot of talking which caused Shun'boo to fall asleep. Shun'boo was awaken by her mom calling her name. She opened her eyes and the doctor was standing at the side of her bed. He told her that her tests results were back. He told her that she had a sinus infection, ear infection, and stomach virus that she had contacted at school. The doctor stated, he would send her home on a special diet for a couple of days with some medication and bed rest for three days. He told her mom that she should be just fine and to make sure she take her medicine as instructed. The doctor told her to follow up with her primary care doctor and ask if she had any questions. Shun'boo's mom said, "Did her pregnancy test come back negative?" He said, "Yes it came back negative." The doctor shook Shun'boo mom hand and Drea hand and told them to take care. He touched Shun'boo shoulder and said, "You will be just fine." He told them that the nurse would be back in the room shortly to bring the discharge papers. Her mom, told the doctor "thank you." Shun'boo mom ask Drea how did he get to the hospital. He told her that his roommate dropped him off. Her mom told Drea that she would take him home. He said that would be great because he wanted to stop by the grocery store to buy Shun'boo the food she need for her strict diet which was ordered by the doctor. He also wanted to pay for her medicine while they were there. Shun'boo mom said, "Ok." There was a knock on the door and as it opened the nurse told them that she had the discharge papers.

She told Shun'boo mom that she was going to remove the IV first, then she would go over the discharge instructions with her. She went over the discharge instructions and told them they were good to go and they need to stop by the discharge window before exiting the hospital. The nurse ask her mom did she know where the discharge window was. Her

CHAPTER 24

Her mom ask Drea did he want to stop by the pharmacy first. Drea said that they could stop by the pharmacy first then they could go to the grocery store. When they got to the pharmacy Drea gave Shun'boo mom the money and ask would it be enough. Her mom said, "Yes." Drea said he would wait in the car with Shun'boo. Drea got out of the car and got in the back seat with Shun'boo. He sat next to her and began rubbing her head. Her mom returned back to the car. Her mom saw that Drea had gotten in the back seat with Shun'boo. She told him he might as well stay back there with her because she knew he would get in the back seat with Shun'boo before arriving at the grocery store. They arrived at the grocery store and Drea asked her mom did she need any more money to get the food Shun'boo need. Her mom told Drea that he had given her enough money for the medicine and the food. Shun'boo thought that her mom should not have to pay for medicine because she has health insurance. Drea gave Shun'boo mom some extra money and ask could she bring him a 12 pack of sodas and some candy. She got the money from him and said she would be right back. While they were sitting in the car Drea told Shun'boo he wanted to talk to her about her smart mouth. Her mom was listening to Drea while closing the car door and said Shun'boo does have a smart mouth. Drea looked over at Shun'boo and said, 'I know everything is not what you want it to be at home." He also told her that she had to forgive her mom and love her pass her faults. He told her that she also had to forgive her stepfather as well.

Shun'boo replied to Drea with anger in her voice saying, "Who are you to tell me about forgiveness." He said to Shun'boo I'm not trying to force you to forgive. He told her that he was asking her to forgive them because he loved them all. However, "SILENCE" filled the car and tears began to fall from Drea eyes. He took Shun'boo head and laid her head on his chest rubbing her head and said, "I will always respect your mom and your stepfather even when they are wrong and everything will be well with you." He ask her to forgive him and he wanted her to know that he truly loved her. He told her every moment they spent together was valuable to him. Shun'boo mom came out the grocery store and Drea got out of the car to help her with the groceries. When Drea got back in the car he told her mom that he would buy a box of chicken for her to take home because he knew she was tired. Her mom told Drea that he didn't have to buy chicken because Shun'boo's stepfather had told her that he would be cooking. Her stepfather wanted some butterbeans. She told Drea she likes how he cook them. Drea said, 'Are you sure?" Shun'boo's mom said, "I'm sure" as they arrived at Drea's house. He told Shun'boo that he wanted her to lay down and get some rest. He kissed her on the forehead and told her to call him if she need anything. He then told her he would call her later to check on her. He told her mom thank you for dropping him off at home and drive safely. Drea stood on the sidewalk watching them pull off waving bye-bye to Shun'boo. She was hoping that her mom wouldn't ask her any questions about him.

As soon as she turned off the street Drea lived on she ask Shun'boo if Drea talked to her about her smart mouth and she was hoping he did. Shun'boo mom told her she hope that she would listen to him because she was not going to have her child being disrespectful. Shun'boo just wanted peace. She said, 'Yes mama," Drea talked to me. She thought how her mom justified all her wrong doing. She thought to herself how her mom would take her anger out on her and her siblings because of their stepfather selfish ways and lack of love for what her mom desired. Shun'boo thought often that how she too desired for her stepfather to love her mom. "Love is not abuse." She thought love is never controlling. "Love is never to dominate a person." Love never steals one identity from another. Love does exactly how it's spelled, pronounced, and what it means "'LOVE." If you spell the word backwards it would be EVOL, which is derived from the word evolve. Shun'boo thought how her stepfather, her mom, and humanity was created to evolve in love. She thought what it would be like if an revolution of love overtook humanity hearts and how the world would be. She thought it would be just what she thought, "LOVE THE GREAT REIGN" what Shun'boo mom had justified as her lack of mothering gift. Her mom was treated so harsh by their stepfather and it began to affect her and her sisters. Her mom had found a way to escape her conscious which reminded her of her wrongs and the escape for her mom was to betray her daughter. As a rebellious child with a sarcastic mouth it was her mom's way of not having to deal with the conscious mind, which is known as common sense that is embedded in every human beings thoughts.

Shun'boo thought how thoughts can be powerful if they can make a person change for the good or better. If a person is changed for the good and the better they will sure live a good life!!! If you are wrong and no one ever told you that you were wrong she felt you will die with your

CHAPTER 25

Her sisters ask her did Drea come up to the hospital because when she called him earlier he was concerned about her. She told her sister that Drea had come to the hospital. Shun'boo ask her sister if she could turn off the bedroom light so she could get some rest. While everyone was eating dinner her sister said, "Yes, I will turn the lights off so you can get some rest. Her sister turn the lights off and Shun'boo was fast asleep. Shun'boo was awaken by her mom. She told her that it was time for her to take her medicine. Her mom told her that she would read the instructions over with her how to take the medicine and after that she could take it on her own. Shun'boo mom knew that she was a smart teenage girl and a responsible girl as well. After her mom had read the instructions on how and when to take the medicine, she told her that after she take her bath she was still expected to clean the bathroom. Her mom told her that she could ask one of her sister's to clean it up for her. Shun'boo said, "Yes mama." After her mom had left the room she got up and went into the den area where her siblings were. They all ask her did she need anything or did she want help with anything. Her siblings' thoughtfulness and care for her made her smile. She told them she loved them all and that she was alright. Shun'boo never wanted to overwhelm her siblings and most of all she definitely did not want them to be in her situation. She told them that she was about to eat. Shun'boo ask them had they taken their baths because she wanted to take her bath after she finished eating.

They said, "Yes." Her sister's ask her what the doctor said. She told them she had a sinus infection, ear infection, and a stomach virus. She told them she could have gotten the stomach virus from school. She told them that she would not sleep in the room with them. Shun'boo decided to sleep in the den on the couch. She also told them that she would miss school for the rest of the week. Shun'boo next to the oldest sister, told her that she hoped that she would be able to get some rest. She smiled and said, "I know" and they laughed. The laughter seemed to change the atmosphere's heaviness that Shun'boo felt. She would feel that heaviness often and overwhelmed with whatever was put on her, which she was never created to carry. It was though she was clothed with garments of heaviness and how she would often think of being set "FREE." While Shun'boo finish eating her soup the house phone rang and it was Drea. Her sister gave her the telephone, Shun'boo said, "hello" in a pleasant but concerned voice. Drea asked, how she was feeling. Shun'boo told Drea that she was tired, she had taken her medicine, and she just finished eating. He asked her did she get any rest. She told Drea yes, she had taken a nap. He told her that he was glad to hear that she had gotten some rest. He told her that he would be coming over to see her Saturday. Besides, he also had to give Shun'boo's sister the money to get her hair done as he had promised. He told Shun'boo if she need anything before then she could reach him at the restaurant or at home. He asked her to leave a message for him if he was unreachable.

She told Drea ok that she was tired and wanted to take a bath. She then told him that she would have to talk to him later. He said, "Alright beautiful, I love you and have a goodnight." Shun'boo hung up the telephone. She would normally tell Drea she love him too. Shun'boo thought how situations whether they were good or bad certainly affected the living conditions of a person and how situations good or bad could change the course of someone's life. Shun'boo help her sisters clean up the kitchen and the dining area after they were finish. She told them that she was going to take a bath. They said they were going to sleep. She told them goodnight just in case they were asleep before she came back in the bedroom. She knew that most of the time that they all would lie in the bed and talk about school or whatever happened in the neighborhood. They also would talk about girl things. Shun'boo got her pajamas and her personal care bag and went to take her bath. She laid there soaking in the warm bubble bath water. She had used dish detergent to make her bubble bath with because she had ran out of bubble bath soap. She thought to herself hoping she didn't throw off her PH balance. Shun'boo began nodding off to sleep while in the bathtub. She knew it was time for her to get out of the bathtub. The bathroom started to fill with steam. The warm bath help her sweat out a lot of the unhealthy bacteria that was in her body. She got out of the bathtub and began to get dressed. She then gathered all of her things and took them and put them where they belong. Next, she gathered the cleaning supplies to clean the bathroom. She made sure she clean the bathroom well.

She didn't want her mom to come and check the bathroom and find out something wasn't clean enough or half cleaned. After she was done cleaning the bathroom she was eager to lay back down. She rechecked the bathroom, turn the lights off and put the cleaning supplies where they belong. She went and checked on her sisters and they all were asleep. She shut the door to the bedroom where they were sleeping.

CHAPTER 26

She said, "I am feeling fine." Shun'boo didn't want to raise any concerns even though she was feeling a little weak. She told them that she would be right back and that she was going to the den to fold up the blankets and put them away. Next, she got some water to take her medicine with. They said, "Ok." Shun'boo stepfather walked in the kitchen and opened the refrigerator to get his lunch that he always prepared at night. He put his lunch in his lunch box that he carried to work. Glancing up at Shun'boo he said, "I heard you were going to shoot hooky from school for a couple of days." She said to her stepfather, "I'm not shooting hooky from school the doctor have me on bed rest for three days because I don't feel well. Her stepfather said to her it was still called shooting hooky to him. Shun'boo finish folding the blankets and put them up. She got a glass of water to take her medicine with. Shun'boo walked back to the room where her sisters were getting dressed for school. Shun'boo re-read the instructions on her medicine before taking it. Their mom came in the room and told them it was time for them to leave out for school so they could eat breakfast at school. Shun'boo and her sister didn't eat breakfast at school. They decided to get something out of the vending machine in the school's gym. Her sisters told her bye. She hugged them and said she will see them later. Off to school they went. Shun'boo started cleaning up their bedroom. She was glad that it was not much to clean. Her sister had already made up her bed. Shun'boo only had to put a few things up where they belong and vacuum the room.

Her mom came in the bedroom and ask her did she take her medicine. She told her mom that she had taken her medicine. Shun'boo ask her mom was there anything that she wanted her to do because she was a bit weak and she wanted to lie down. Her mom told her she could lie down and rest. Her mom told her she could make sure the bathroom was clean after she get some rest. Shun'boo said, "Yes mama" while pulling the covers back from the bed that was made up perfect by her sisters. They all would make up the bed together. It would be two of them on each side of the bed. Two of them at the head of the bed and the other two of them at the foot of the bed. They would shake the sheet well because one of her sisters were told at school that bed bugs can get in your bed if you go outside and play and don't take a bath afterwards. If the bedbugs get in your clothes you would infect the bed with bedbugs. Shun'boo had told her sister that was a made up tale. She didn't want her sister to be afraid to sleep at night. Shun'boo liked shaking the white sheets which reminded her of a beautiful white cloud. She got in the bed and thought about Drea. She thought about how he hurt her with his betrayal and how he took care of her at the same time. Shun'boo fell asleep. She was awaken by the sound of the vacuum cleaner. She laid there in the bed knowing that it was her mom cleaning and vacuuming her bedroom. Shun'boo and her sisters' bedroom door was slightly closed, but when the bedroom door was swung open it was her baby brother.

He was one of the most beautiful toddlers she had seen. Shun'boo loved him unconditionally. She took good care of him and even Drea adored him. He was a spoiled child. Everyone spoiled him. Shun'boo stepfather, mother, and siblings all spoiled him. He walked up the side of the bed and extended his hand towards Shun'boo. She picked him up. She held him close in her arms giving him countless kisses on his cheek. She began tickling him on the side of his abdomen. He burst out with laughter and made her feel happy. Indeed, he was a spoil, and loveable child. He played no role in spoiling himself because he was too little to decipher what was spoiled and not being spoiled. They all loved him and people thought that her baby brother was Drea's and Shun'boo's child because they always carried him with them. They would buy him whatever they wanted him to have. Her mom came in the room looking for him. She told Shun'boo to put him down because she didn't want him to catch the stomach virus that she had. Shun'boo said, "Yes mama." She gave her brother another kiss on his cheek and put him down. She stood him gently on the floor by the bed where she was laying. Her mom took him by the hands and walked him out of the room. As Shun'boo mom was leaving out of the bedroom she told Shun'boo to clean the bathroom. She got up and out of the bed and went to get the cleaning supplies to clean the bathroom. After she was done cleaning she re-checked everything in the bathroom to make sure everything was clean perfect. She turned off the lights and went to put the cleaning supplies where they belong. She had gotten hungry.

She warmed her some soup and ate some saltine crackers which seem to help with the nausea she was experiencing. After she finish eating she drank a glass of water and clean everything up again. She went and stood outside under the carport and took a deep breathe breathing in the fresh midmorning air. She enjoyed smelling the morning fresh air especially when they would walk to the bus stop on their way to school in the morning. As she was standing outside she saw some teenagers walking down the street together laughing and talking. She thought

CHAPTER 27

Shun'boo had observed that quality about Drea. The tone in his voice was the perfect dialogue and well- chosen words. He could make anybody want to hold a conversation with him. Shun'boo noticed that was why people enjoyed and confided in Drea. He was a great listener. He was never judgmental and Shun'boo could see why males confided in Drea just as he had already mentioned to her. Drea ask her how has she been feeling. She said, that it would never be the same between the two of them. Drea told her that he agreed with her and that with time it would be revealed why their paths crossed. Shun'boo had heard someone wise say, "Life has many paths that you can take, but the wise one would take the straight and narrow path. Its path will lead you to the good path of life." She thought what did Drea mean when he mentioned that to her. He told her that she didn't have to call to the restaurant to let the manager know she was sick and would be out for a couple of days because he had already done so. The manager who was part owner of the restaurant knew Drea well and he was liked by the managers. Shun'boo told Drea that she was tired and that she was about to lie down. He told her he loved her and for her to rest well and he would call her later in the night. When she hung up the telephone it was time for her to take her medicine again. She fixed a glass of water and went into the bedroom to get her medicine. After she had finish taking her medicine she laid down in the bed thinking again about what Drea had said to her earlier. While trying to compress her thoughts with other things she had drifted off to sleep.

She was awakened by her sisters calling her name, "Shun'boo." As she opened her eyes she was glad to see them. It seem they had a busy day because their hair was a bit messy. It was not as neatly well-combed as before they left for school that morning. She said, "Hi" to them. She ask them how was their day. They told her they had fun at school because the school had a picnic lunch for all students and after they were done eating they could play. Shun'boo thought to herself that explains why their hair was messy. She said that was wonderful. They ask her how she felt. She told them that she was feeling a little bit better. They said, "Hey." They loved their big sister. Shun'boo laying in the bed thinking it shouldn't be long before her other sister arrived home. The other sibling and Shun'boo always arrived home after their other siblings because their school was a street over behind their house. Her sisters and she were talking about all the fun they had at school. Her other sister arrived home. Shun'boo was happy to see her. She ask her how was her day at school. Her sister told her it seem to be a long day. Shun'boo said, "Is everything alright? Her sister said, "Yes." Shun'boo ask, "Did you miss me?" Her sister smile and said, "Girl, yes." Shun'boo laughed. Her other sisters were changing their clothes. Shun'boo laid there thinking while talking with them and watching them how she would come home from school and take off her clothes and change into what their mom called play clothes. It was the clothes that were considered not so nice to wear in public. They were old worn out clothes, but still suitable to wear in the house.

They all finish changing their clothes and they started on their homework. Shun'boo next to the oldest sister said she had quite a bit of homework to do and she had to get started. Shun'boo ask her sister did she need any help. Her sister said, "No' that she was good. Shun'boo said, "alright and let me know if you change your mind. I will help you with any of your homework assignments except math." Math was Shun'boo least favorite school subject and it was not her greatest strength. Her sister said, "I know you don't enjoy math." Shun'boo said, "How do you know that." Her sister said, "Because you tell me that when we pass each other in the hallway at school while you are preparing to go to your math class. Shun'boo, said "Oh Yea I Forget" and they both laughed. Their mom came into the room as she normally would to make sure everyone was at home and had changed their school clothes and began on their homework. Her sisters were all spread out laying on the floor doing their homework. Her younger sisters ask their mom when they finish their homework could they go outside and play. She told them yes. She told Shun'boo to check their work and make sure they finish it before they went outside to play. Shun'boo said, 'Yes mama." She told her sisters while they were finishing their homework that she would be getting her bath. Shun'boo gathered her things and went to take her bath. While soaking in the tub she thought about going back to school. She also thought about the girl who had come up to her in the restroom and would the girl come to her with something else or provoke her in anyway.

Shun'boo didn't stay in the bath tub long even though she wanted to soak for a while to sweat out some of the toxins in her body. She knew she had to take a quicker bath than usual because she had to check her sister's homework. Her mom would always check her brother's homework even though he never really needed any help with his homework. He was a

CHAPTER 28

They said, "Yes." Her next to the oldest sister was still laying on the floor completing her homework. Her other sister came back in the room from the kitchen. Shun'boo ask her did she wash the glass out and put the glass in the dish rack to dry. She said, "Yes." Shun'boo told them to give her their homework. She checked their homework and she told all of them they could go outside except her youngest sister because she had not completed her English homework entirely and it was not correct. She had to help her with it. Their baby sister ask, could they wait on her before they went outside to play. Shun'boo said, "Depending on how long it would take her to finish. Shun'boo also stated she should not take long with completing her work only about 10 more minutes at the most. She told them she only had to change five questions to make the answers correct. They said, "How about if we just go outside and see if our friends are outside playing and let them know we can come outside today to play and then we will come back and see if she is finished with her homework. Shun'boo said, "That sounds good." She ask her sister to re-read the questions that she had gotten incorrect and then reselect the correct answer. After her sister had reread the questions and Shun'boo instructing her to listen carefully she got the answers correct. Her other sisters came in the house and ask was she finish. Their youngest sister yelled, "Yes" expressing her excitement to go outside and play. They left to go outside and play. Shun'boo said for them to be careful and that they were to watch their younger sister. They said, "Ok we will." Shun'boo ask her next to the oldest sister how for a long she was before completing her homework.

She said that she only had the subject she was working on and the one other subject. After that Shun'boo told her sister that she would be quiet and not talk to her so she could get finish with her homework. Shun'boo got up to go the kitchen to get something to drink. The money that Drea had given her mom to buy Shun'boo some food and something to drink was spent on ginger ale for her to drink. Shun'boo knew that the ginger ale was for her because the only time her mom would buy it if someone in the home was sick with an upset stomach. The ginger ale would help to settle their stomach. Her stepfather had come home from work. Shun'boo said, "Hi' to her stepfather making sure she spoke where he could hear her. If she didn't speak or her voice was very low, he and her mom would think she didn't want to speak to him and she was being disrespectful. They never considered the low tone in her voice when she spoke to her stepfather, which was a teenaged girl whose spirit was broken. Shun'boo was a teenaged girl who was often sad but compressed it to protect them. Shun'boo stepfather said, "Hey how did it feel to have been able to do nothing all day." Shun'boo thought do nothing all day, he already knew that she wouldn't be able to fully lie down the entire day. She told her stepfather that she didn't lie down the entire day that she had to clean up. Her stepfather said, "Well, that was good that your mom had you up and moving about because laying in the bed can only prolong you from getting better." Shun'boo thought to herself that the doctor had advised her mom of Shun'boo care, which was for her to rest in bed for three days.

Besides, she thought that she was weak, tired, and nauseated. She knew her body needed the rest and her body was letting her know that she needed rest. Shun'boo had never slept that much before even when she would try to fight her sleep. Her body was letting her know that it had been deprived of sleep even before Shun'boo had gotten sick. She thought that her stepfather and mother knew she needed to be resting in the bed. Shun'boo washed the glass and put it in the dishrack to dry. She went back into the bedroom to see was her sister finish with her homework. Her sister had fallen asleep on the floor. She was sleeping peacefully. Shun'boo took the blanket that they had on their bed that always stayed folded and placed it at the foot of the bed whenever they make the bed in the mornings. She took the blanket and placed it over her sister. She didn't want to wake her up. Shun'boo enjoyed seeing her sisters and brother rest. Her youngest brother had not become of age to help clean the house. Her stepfather and mom was over excessive with harsh rules and punishment no matter what it was or concerned. Shun'boo turned the lights off in the bedroom. Their bedroom seem to not get as much light from the day light as the other bedrooms would. It had to be really sunny to get a good quality of light in their bedroom. Shun'boo laid across the bed thinking she would lay down until her siblings came in the house from their play time. She knew it wouldn't be long because they had spent most of their time doing their homework. She laid there thinking about her job at the restaurant and how she enjoyed working at her job.

She also thought about the fact that she could make extra money to help buy her siblings things they needed and wanted, but it was becoming a bit too much. She thought from getting up going to school, cleaning up before she left for school in the mornings and at the same time trying to get herself dressed and get to the bus stop to catch the bus was a lot

CHAPTER 29

She would take the blame for everything if she was home at that particular time because she knew her stepfather and mother would punish her siblings and her for it. Shun'boo thought how she could never understand the harsh punishment her stepfather and mother would inflict on her. She thought maybe she was despised by them both because of their actions toward her which led her to think such. Shun'boo thought about all that they had inflicted on her mentally, emotionally, and physically. Shun'boo thought about all the times she would run out of the house to escape the cruel punishment. She knew she had to endure the punishment from their stepfather and mother because of the love she had for her siblings. All of them living in a house where they saw how their stepfather would bestow, abuse, and show selfish acts on their mom and their mom neglecting them and herself out of desperation for unconditional love, commitment, respect, trust and faithfulness from their stepfather. Shun'boo would say many times how she wanted them to unite in the unity of pure love between each other and themselves. She thought about how it would be to live in a "HOME" where love dwells and to encounter the presence of love in their "HOME." She thought what it would be like and feel like to be given unconditional love from her stepfather and mother. Shun'boo thought how the love she had for them was never enough for them. She always tried to love and respect her stepfather despite all his mental, physical, and emotional abuse. She thought about how she loved her mom more than she could ever know and Shun'boo showed her love for her mom by being respectful, protecting, and helping her when her stepfather would beat her. Shun'boo would make sure they didn't lack for any necessities.

She worked and she helped her mom with the bills and Drea also contributed. Shun'boo thought how she would take care of her sisters and brothers. Everything she did for them was because she loved them "HER FAMILY" unconditionally. The only thing she wanted from her stepfather and mother was "LOVE." Shun'boo thought where abuse is present and love is replaced in its place then all forms of abuse will be eradicated. Shun'boo's siblings had come back in from playing outside. They had to be in the house before the outside street lights came on and if the streets lights come on and you were not in the house you were grounded. Shun'boo thought how she would get grounded for not making sure her siblings got home before the street lights came on. Shun'boo was crying out for help, but no one took notice. She thought only if they would have looked in her eyes where her physical well-being of a person could be seen. Shun'boo thought it was fascinating to know that a person has a pulse and breathing, but is unresponsive. Why do a medical professional person always look and examine an unresponsive person's eyes. The reason for examining the eyes will show the well-being of a person when they can't speak. Shun'boo thought about being separated from her siblings if she spoke about what she was enduring inside the enclosed walls of their house, but if you looked in her eyes carefully her eyes would have told you her well-being. Shun'boo thought how people would ask whoever they were talking to; to look them in their eyes. Looking someone in the eyes was a form of connectivity. She even thought how people would ask someone who they were talking with to look them in their eyes, especially if they suspected the person was being untruthful to them.

The eyes would reveal truth and lies. Shun'boo thought the eyes also were powerful "Be Careful what you cast Your EYES UPON AND ADMIRE IT." Shun'boo next to the oldest sister had awaken from her nap. She said to Shun'boo why didn't you wake me up? She told her sister because you were sleeping peacefully and I didn't want to wake you. Her sister asked her what time it was. Shun'boo told her sister she didn't know but they had to start preparing for school. All of her siblings started to prepare for school for the following day. Shun'boo could smell food being cooked because the aroma was coming from the kitchen into their bedroom. She knew her stepfather or mother was cooking dinner. The house phone rang. Her mom came in the room and told her that Drea was on the phone and that she had to come in the den to talk with him. Shun'boo thought what she did to have to talk to Drea in the den because she was allowed to talk to Drea in the bedroom and she was not on a punishment. Shun'boo said, "Yes, mama." She followed her mom out the bedroom. Her mom picked the cordless telephone off the counter and handed it to her. Shun'boo said, "Drea" saying his name as to let him know she knew it was him on the phone. He said, "Hi beautiful, how are you feeling?" She told Drea she was doing fine while side eyeing her stepfather and mother while they were standing in the kitchen cooking as though they were listening to her conversation with Drea at the same time. She was trying to pick up on their energy because he stepfather and mother would give off a strong energy when they were about to punish her.

If the energy came from only one of them the energy would be lesser than when the energy was coming from them both simultaneously. The energy always felt evil and dark and reminded her of the dreams she would have falling in a black hole and look around for help. Before she hit the bottom in her dream a great but gentle force would always take hold of her and bring her safely back to the top out of the dark hole. Shun'boo told Drea that she had to get off the phone because she had to take her medicine and she was going to sleep after she ate dinner. Drea ask her was she ok. Shun'boo said, "Yes, thanks for asking and goodnight." She hung up the telephone and she could feel the evil energy coming from the kitchen to the den. Shun'boo thought as she was walking off when will they embark their harsh punishment towards her. They knew that she was too weak to defend herself or run away to escape from them, at least for a while because she didn't have her full vitality because she was sick. She knew it wouldn't be long before they punished her because when that evil energy was present it would not strike until a day or a couple of days later. Her mom said, "Miss Shun'boo we will be dealing with you later." She said, "Yes mama" trying to stall them not giving them any reason to punish her that night. Shun'boo crying in the inside because she didn't want her siblings to again witness their harsh punishment towards her. She didn't want to see anymore tears fall from their eyes because of the cruel punishment. Shun'boo went into the bedroom and laid across the bed and the thoughts began flooding her mind how her mom would have her to remove her clothes.

CHAPTER 30

However, her mom allowed her to keep her bra on even removing her panties while she beat her. She made her lay stretched out on the bed until she was tired and if her stepfather and mother beat her together her mom would always start first, then her mom would give the thick leather belt to her stepfather and saying at the same time "beat her, beat her" until she cries. Shun'boo hearing her stepfather saying you are not going to cry. She had developed an inner strength as she became an adolescent and that inner strength friend name was Rambo. She would appear at Shun'boo pinnacle point of anger. She never liked to see her appear. She was a fighter with no fear never giving in to defeat. Shun'boo remember hearing the yelling and crying asking her stepfather and mother to stop. Shun'boo never shed a tear, looking her siblings in their eyes with love. As she thought she was being beaten harshly she didn't want them to ever endure this kind of cruel punishment, especially from the ones who supposed to love them. They were a gift given to them. She thought what situation had arisen for them to want to punish her this time. She thought it couldn't be the lights because she had trained her thoughts to remember to cut them off in the bathroom. It was something about leaving the bathroom light on that seem to anger her stepfather and mother. She thought did she forget to do something around the house, but she knew it couldn't be possible because she always wanted to please them, meet their satisfaction, and become a master of the "TO DO ALL list" always wanting to have peace with them and in the house. Shun'boo siblings were finish getting prepared for school for the next day.

Her stepfather call them all by their individual names to come and eat dinner. Shun'boo stayed in the room even though she was not able to eat what had been prepared by her stepfather. She had been placed on a strict diet by the doctor. She didn't have an appetite to eat anything. Shun'boo knew she lost a few pounds and some inches because her clothes were fitting her looser than before she had gotten sick. She hoped that they all got done eating dinner and cleaning up so she could lie down to go to sleep. She thought how she just wanted to sleep away the pain and not have to face the life she was presently living with. Her siblings had finished eating dinner when her next to the oldest sister came in the bedroom and told her that their mom said that she had to help clean the kitchen. Shun'boo got up and followed her sister to the kitchen. She was glad her stepfather and mom had gone in their bedroom. They would most of the time eat their dinner in their bedroom and very seldom eat in the den on the couch. Shun'boo help her sisters clean the kitchen. Her next to the oldest sister asked her what had happened with a puzzled look. Shun'boo asked her sister why she ask her what happened. Her sister told her that she overheard their stepfather and mother saying they were going to deal with her. Shun'boo knew that meant punish her. She told her sister that she didn't do anything just as she had never done anything that cause them to inflict harsh punishment on her. She told her sister don't worry that she would be alright. Shun'boo told her sister 'You know that I love you." Her sister said, "Yes I love you too sister" standing in the den of their house.

They embraced each other with a hug of pure and genuine sister love. However, that is the kind of love that should be felt between all sisters and siblings. Shun'boo and her sister were close and always there for each other. She told her sister that she was going to lie down and get some rest even if she didn't get any sleep that night. Furthermore, as she thought to herself would her stepfather and mother wake her or would her thoughts keep her up. After all, her body was extremely tired. She went into the bedroom and said, "Goodnight" to her sisters. Then she went into the other bedroom adjacent to the bedroom she shared with her other sisters and told her brother and younger sister Goodnight. Shun'boo younger sister came and hugged her and gave her a kiss on the cheek. Her youngest sister loved her because Shun'boo had spoiled her as well. She told them don't forget to turn off the lights and to use the bathroom before they got into bed to go to sleep. They both said, "Ok." Shun'boo went and used the bathroom so she wouldn't have to get up and use it later on that night. Normally, she didn't have to get up in the night to use the bathroom if she used it before lying down for bedtime only if she avoided not drinking a lot of liquids before going to sleep. She went into the laundry room to get the blankets she had previously used the night before. She laid down saying out loud "I just want to sleep peacefully," but not loud enough for her to be heard by anyone in the house. She closed her eyes and before she knew it a new day came. Shun'boo heard the birds chirping as though they were singing songs of a new day.

Shun'boo shaking her head trying to gain full conscious with her baby brother pulling on her clothes trying to pull himself up onto her. She looked at him and said, "Good morning," giving him a warm smile. She then picked him up. Her brother laid his head right below her shoulder and chest. She kissed his cheeks and ask him was he ready to eat. She

CHAPTER 31

They all finish doing their last bit of touch ups to themselves, got their book bags, and left the house going to school. Shun'boo and her baby brother following behind them telling them bye as they were walking from the house. Her mother opening the door telling her to bring her brother back inside and to give him to her because she still had a stomach virus. Shun'boo walk back into the house. Her mom was in the kitchen cooking breakfast for her brother. She went into the bedroom to get her medicine to take. She thought she would wait until her mom finish cooking before going into the kitchen to get something to eat. She decided to clean up the bedroom although it was not much to clean. Her sisters and her always kept the room clean and they had already made the bed up before leaving for school. She put a few things away and got her some comfortable clothes to put on after she takes her bath. She was so glad to get a warm bath. She didn't have any bubble bath and was not going into the kitchen to get the dish soap. She decided to take the soap and lather it up placing the soap under the running water to create bubbles for the bath water. She laid back in the tub hoping she could relax without her mom beating on the door telling her to hurry up. She thought how her body could use detoxing and get that bad bacteria out of her body. Besides, she thought she should take a quick bath the other day to help her sisters with their homework so they could go outside and play. Shun'boo laid there thinking that her stepfather had left for work early that morning. This particular morning she didn't see him come into the kitchen to get his lunch.

Shun'boo said that she had to really be in a deep sleep. While laughing to herself she said, "I wonder if I was sleeping peacefully as she had seen her siblings do." Shun'boo was able to soak and detox sweating out a lot of impurities in her body. As she was drying off her mom came beating on the door telling her to get out and that she better not run all of the water because she was not going to pay a high water bill. Shun'boo said, "Yes mama, I'm already out and I'm getting dressed." Her mom said, "I want you to vacuum the den and both of the bedrooms. She said, "Yes mama." Shun'boo finish getting dressed and put her things where they belong and clean the bathroom rechecking everything. The bathroom was clean. She turn off the lights and went to put up the cleaning supplies. Shun'boo thinking she needed to take her medicine. She fixed a glass of water and went into the bedroom to get her medicine to take. She went into the kitchen to wash the glass and get the vacuum. She had vacuumed her younger brother and sister room last. Shun'boo turned the vacuum off because she heard her mom talking on the telephone. She could hear her mom saying she will be returning back to school on Monday and that she had called the school's office already to let them know that her daughter was going to be out for three days. However, the doctor had put her on bed rest for a few days and that she will have a signed doctor excuse when she return. She also heard her mom say, "You have a good day as well," but with an unpleasant tone in her voice. As Shun'boo finish wrapping the cord around the vacuum cleaner she could hear her mom speaking out loud.

Her mom was saying to herself that she didn't know why the school was calling her house. Furthermore, she had already called them to let them know that Shun'boo was going to be out of school and that they were being nosey as always. Shun'boo was thinking to herself that even the nice things seem to somehow make her mom mad. Shun'boo thought it was nice for someone from the school to call and check on her to see how she was feeling. After she had put the vacuum cleaner up she warmed her some soup and ate some saltine crackers. She enjoyed eating soup and crackers when she was not sick. Shun'boo enjoyed eating soup and sandwiches also. She finish eating then cleaned everything up. She was not tired as she had been the previous days before. She went into the bedroom and laid across the bed. Shun'boo thinking what she could do to occupy some time until her siblings come home from school. She got up to get her new journal book which she had not written anything in it. Shun'boo thinking she would write expressing her love for her family making sure she thought to keep it all positive because the last journal she had was when she was much younger. However, her grandmother on her biological father side had bought it for her as a Christmas gift. Shun'boo didn't see her dad much often growing up. Her sister and she only saw him mostly around the holidays and sometimes in the summer. When they did see him they enjoyed spending time with him and seeing their other family. Shun'boo resembled a lot like her dad and so did her sister in some ways. Her sister and she didn't know the real truth why they were not able to see their dad and their other family as often.

Shun'boo father was unaware what was going on from all the harsh treatment from her stepfather and mom. Her sister and her always made sure they never raise any suspension that something was wrong even when their father would ask them if everything was alright and was her sister being treated right. They would always say "Yes." Shun'boo

CHAPTER 32

She notice while sitting in the pews at church that behind each row of pews was bibles and books that had hymns written in them that she had heard the congregation and her grandmother sing. Shun'boo had the hymns book in her hand glancing down at it she followed along with the congregation singing the hymns as well. The church choir and congregation sounded angelic. Shun'boo got the bible out of the bucket and laid across the bed to read. As she opened the bible it went directly to Psalm 24:1-7. She read the entire Psalm. The first verse kept resonating in her thoughts. Shun'boo began to have deep thoughts that the world she lived in belonged to GOD and she too belonged to GOD. There was an overwhelming presence of peace that came over her all of sudden and tears began to flow like a creek from her face. The flowing was like spring water. As thoughts began to flood her mind showing her that this is GOD and what she was reading about was the same GOD who helped her out of that dark deep hole that she had fallen in. GOD took hold of her and brought her out to safety. Shun'boo began crying out "OH GOD, MY GOD" repeatedly as her spirit began to quiet down she heard a small voice say "I Love You Shun'boo and I also love your stepfather and mother, and I ask you to love them; I will never leave or forsake you. I'm always with you." Shun'boo said, with a yielded heart to

GOD and a committed heart that she would love them. She knew that day that something had changed for the better for her and her stepfather and mother. They were not aware of GOD's unconditional love for them both and they were created by him and for him for his glory.

Shun'boo drifted off to sleep with her bible in her arms. Shun'boo was awaken by the smell of food cooking. The aroma was a pleasing smell. It smelled liked barbeque chicken and black eyed peas with the smell of tea brewing. Shun'boo thought what time it was as she was getting up. She saw her bible still by her side. She got her bible and placed it back in her special bucket and closed the lid back down. She smiled as she put the bible away thinking about what happened between God and her. She had to use the bathroom because her bladder was full. She grabbed her medicine off of the dresser as she was leaving out the bedroom. After Shun'boo had relieved her bladder she washed her hands and open her medicine and took it with some hydrate sink water. She used her hands to fill water in them once the inside of her palms were filled with enough water she sipped the water from her hands to take her medicine. Shun'boo dried the sink off with some tissue and flushed it. She then turned the light off and went into the kitchen to get her something to eat. She thought that it would be nice to drink some ginger ale. Shun'boo taste buds were craving something else besides water. She glanced over at the stove and her mom had the food cooking on low. The food smelled great knowing that she couldn't eat it because of her three day diet the doctor had put her on. Shun'boo smiling to herself thinking she was glad that it was her last day for her to be on the restricted diet. She warmed her some soup up and poured her a glass of ginger ale and sat at the dining room table to eat.

However, when she was done eating she heard laughing and talking and the sound of buses. She said, "I know school is not already out looking at the kitchen clock. Shun'boo said time flew by today. The children had gotten out of school. She got up from the table to wash the dishes that she had used and clean the dining table. Shun'boo was making dish water in the sink when she heard knocking at the door. She knew it was her siblings because Shun'boo heard their voices talking to each other while they were waiting for someone to open the door. Shun'boo opened the door smiling at them. She said, "Hey you all how was your day?" Her siblings said that they all had a good day. Shun'boo taking her hands messing with her sister's hair. She told them it was nice that they didn't come home today with their hair messed up. Her sisters and she started to laugh knowing that Shun'boo enjoyed teasing and playing with them. Her sister said that the food sure smelled good and they could smell the aroma of the food as they were walking up to the house. Her sister went into the bedroom. They asked her was she coming in behind them because they had to tell her what had happened at school that day. Shun'boo told them that she would be in the room once she finished cleaning up. Shun'boo mom came into the kitchen just as she had finish cleaning up. Her mom told her to let her siblings know that once they were done changing their school clothes to wash the dirty clothes she had separated earlier that day. Shun'boo mom told her to help them and once the clothes were finish drying for them to fold them and put them away immediately.

Shun'boo said, "Yes mama." Her mom was still in the kitchen checking on the food that she was cooking for dinner. Shun'boo went into the laundry room to see how many dirty loads of clothes they had to wash. Shun'boo sighed a sound of relief glad that they only had two loads of dirty laundry to wash. She went into the bedroom where her sisters were

CHAPTER 33

They all laughed. Shun'boo told them that they had to wash and fold up laundry. Shun'boo told them that she would get started washing while they start on their homework. Her sisters said they didn't have any homework. Shun'boo next to the oldest sister said she had to write a one page essay and that it shouldn't take her long. Her other sister told Shun'boo since she is going to start washing the clothes that they would watch television. Shun'boo started the first load of laundry up and went and sat in the den with her sisters. They ask Shun'boo was it a special day for their stepfather and mother because their mom had cooked dinner and she had cooked dinner on a Friday. She told them she was unaware of a special day. Shun'boo thinking that her mom might had cooked a surprise dinner meal hoping he would not go out that weekend. The house telephone rang and Shun'boo answered the telephone and said, "Hello." It was Drea. He spoke to her by calling her beautiful. Shun'boo said to Drea, how did you know that it was me. Drea laughed and said, how could he not know that angel voice. Shun'boo smiled and ask Drea what did he want. He told her that he was calling to see how she was feeling. She told Drea that she was feeling better. He told her that everyone at the restaurant had ask about her. Shun'boo told Drea that it was nice that they had ask about her. She told Drea that she would be returning back to work on Monday. He told her that if she need to take more time off that it was alright because the manager had told him to let her know. Shun'boo told Drea, "Thank you for letting me know."

He told her that he would be working a short day and when he got off work he would come over her house to see her and give the money to her sister to get her hair done. Shun'boo told Drea she had to finish washing clothes and she would see him tomorrow. Drea told Shun'boo he loved her and she hung up the telephone. Her sisters were still sitting in the den watching television. Shun'boo told her sister that Drea was coming over tomorrow to give her the money to get her hair done. Shun'boo sister said, she was glad because she was tired of the jerry curl. Shun'boo went in the laundry room to put the first load of clothes in the dryer. She loaded the last load of clothes in the washing machine and went to the room. Her next to the oldest sister was on the telephone talking. Shun'boo was speaking very low so whoever her sister was talking too wouldn't hear her as she ask her sister to come in the den when she got off the telephone. Her sister looking directly at her mouth to hear what she was saying. As Shun'boo was leaving the bedroom she heard her sister say to the person she was on the phone with that if they confront my sister about Drea they will have me to deal with. Shun'boo turned around and sat on the bed. Her sister said to the person on the telephone I will talk to you later and hung up the telephone. Shun'boo ask her sister who was that she was talking to on the phone. Her sister told her that it was one of her friends that attended school with them. She told Shun'boo that she had called her friend because she had ask her to call her earlier that day at school.

While changing classes her friend told her that she had something important to tell her. Shun'boo ask her sister what was it that your friend had to tell you. She said, her friend told her she overheard some girls talking about Shun'boo while she was using the restroom at school. One of the girls said that they were going to confront her about her boyfriend that Shun'boo was talking too. Her sister said if that girl or her friends want to fight then a fight they will get. Shun'boo told her sister not to worry because she was not going to worry either. Shun'boo ask her sister to come and help her with the laundry. Shun'boo took the clothes out of the dryer and began folding them up while her sister put the last load of clothes in the dryer to dry. Her sister helped her fold the clothes up. Shun'boo ask her sister did she believe in God. Her sister said, "Yes I believe in God." She told her sister that she believe in God as well. Shun'boo sister ask her did she think that God knew what was going on with all of them. Shun'boo smiled at her sister and said, "Yes he knows what is going on." Her sister said how you know that. She told her sister that while she was at home earlier that day that she had encountered the presence of God and that God had told her that he was with her and has always been and that he will never leave her. Shun'boo told her sister that God had said to her that he loved her and he loved their stepfather and mother. Her sister ask her how could God love them after all the wrong things they both had done.

Her sister said to Shun'boo especially what they have done to you all these years. She told her sister that she knew that God didn't like some of their stepfather and mother's choices, but that didn't stop him from loving them both. Shun'boo told her sister that because of the harden of their stepfather and mother's heart for whatever reason it caused them to get to that place in their lives. Shun'boo told her sister that their stepfather and mother would continually to make those choice because they had not received God in their hearts and they had no fellowship with him. Shun'boo told her sister that the only way that their stepfather

CHAPTER 34

Shun'boo mom came in the room while they were putting the clothes away and told them when they were done putting up the clothes to wash their hands and fix their brother and sister a dinner plate to eat. Shun'boo middle sister came and ask her was she done yet with putting the clothes up. Their mom had come in the den to check on them and told them that Shun'boo and her sister was going to fix her and their other siblings a dinner plate. Shun'boo said to her sister, "yes we are finish putting up the clothes and I'm following right behind you to fix your dinner plate Miss Piggy." She told her sister because you like to pig out when you eat. Shun'boo and her sister laughed. Shun'boo told her sister don't take me serious it's just a figure of speech. Shun'boo grabbed her sister hugging her while shaking her side to side in her arms saying, "you know I have a sense of humor right." Her sister said, "Yes we all know that because of all those lame jokes you tell us." Shun'boo letting her sister go out of her arms told her that if she thought her jokes were not funny that she would be funny by putting a very small portion of food on her dinner plate. Shun'boo sister said, "Ok that's not funny." Their next to the oldest sister said, "ok you all stop playing around so we can eat dinner and then we all can watch a movie together and after we are all done eating we will finish cleaning up the kitchen." All of

Shun'boo siblings looked at her and ask her at the same time as though they were a church choir singing in unison and harmony was she going to watch a movie with them.

They all knew that Shun'boo never really cared to watch television only when their stepfather and mother would allow them to watch a movie which was considered to be free time in their house. Shun'boo would use that time too just lay down thinking with her peaceful thoughts. She told her sister, yes she would watch a movie with them. They all said, "Yay" some of us can lay on the couch and the rest of us can spread a blanket out and lay on the floor. Shun'boo said, "That sounds good now let us fix you all a dinner plate and after everyone is done eating and cleaning up we all will watch the movie. Shun'boo thought to herself how she was glad that this was her last night having to eat soup even though she enjoyed eating soup she wanted to eat desired choices of food. He siblings got done eating their dinner in no time. Shun'boo asked her siblings you all are done eating already. They said, "yes we were hungry and you already know that we ate lunch early in the afternoon, therefore when we got home we were hungry and wanted a snack until dinner was ready. Shun'boo said, "I know right," it was her way of agreeing to what they said. They all cleaned everything back up and got their blankets to watch the movie. Shun'boo told them since she was the oldest she would pick the movie for them to watch. They all told her that it was not fair that she could solely pick the movie for them. They all thought they should vote together on what movie to watch. Shun'boo said, "Alright we all can vote on what movie to watch, but we are not watching any scary movies and if we are watching a movie that has a kissing scene in it you all are to turn your heads until they are done kissing."

Shun'boo next to the oldest sister said," I know you are not talking about me." Shun'boo told her sister, "Yes mama that applies to you also." Her sister said, "Girl you are one year older than me." Shun'boo said to her sister and what does that supposed to mean. Her sister told her that meant, if she had to turn her head at a kissing scene in a movie she had to as well. They all started laughing. They all were looking at the movie channel and they saw a comedy movie that got their interest. After they had read the heading of the movie. Shun'boo turned the television to the channel. They all laughed through the entire movie. Shun'boo heard a car pulling up in the driveway and she could see the car lights reflecting in the house through the side sliding doors. She knew that was her stepfather pulling in. The movie had her sisters and brother undivided attention except her next to the oldest sister. She looked over to Shun'boo with a look on her face to say our stepfather is here. Shun'boo thinking he likely wouldn't come in the house and say anything to her sisters and brother because he would be too focus on getting ready to get cleaned up to go out for the weekend as he normally would. Shun'boo mom came in the kitchen just as her stepfather was entering the house. He spoke to her mom and her mom spoke back with little enthusiasm. Her stepfather looked over at them and ask what they were doing. Shun'boo and her siblings said watching a movie. Shun'boo and her sisters spoke to him after he had ask what they were doing. Her stepfather went to the back and their mom told them to keep the noise down because she could hear them in her bedroom.

Shun'boo thought how her mom related laughter to noise. They all said," Yes mama." Shun'boo looked over at the kitchen clock and it was time for her to take her medicine. As she went into the kitchen and poured her a glass of water she could hear her stepfather and mother arguing. She knew they were arguing about him going out. Shun'boo

CHAPTER 35

Shun'boo reminded them to turn off the bedroom light before they lay down to go to sleep. Shun'boo checked the back door to make sure it was locked. She laid down on the couch thinking to herself what she had heard her stepfather say. She thought what had happened or what was said for her stepfather to say she had a smart mouth. She knew that her stepfather was saying she had a sarcastic mouth. Shun'boo thought was that her stepfather way of getting out of the argument with her mom or to get her mom to back off him to keep him from going out every weekend. She heard the front door open then close and the door knob lock. Shun'boo closed her eyes to get some sleep hoping her mom wouldn't come and wake her about what her stepfather had told her mom to talk to her about. Shun'boo already knew that it wouldn't be no more talking and that it would escalate into harsh punishment for her, especially since her mom was already angry at her stepfather for going out to party and satisfy his fleshly desires. Shun'boo had drifted off to sleep awaken by the sound of the front door opening. The front door had a very distinctive sound when you opened it. She glanced at the clock hanging on the kitchen wall to see what time it was. She knew that was her stepfather coming in because he always got back around the same time when he went out every weekend. Shun'boo closed her eyes to go back to sleep and as soon as she had closed her eyes she heard yelling from her mom. Shun'boo got up running to her stepfather and mother bedroom. She open the door and her stepfather was beating her mom and her mom trying to fight him off her.

Shun'boo grabbed her baby brother up as she turned around to take him out the room to give him to her sisters they all were running up towards the room. Shun'boo gave him to her middle sister and said for her to take him in their bedroom. Shun'boo ran back into the bedroom grabbing her stepfather off her mom and her next to the oldest sister helping her by pulling him off their mom. Shun'boo stood in front of her mom to protect her while her sister was helping their mom up. Shun'boo would always be ready to protect her mom so he would not continuously try to beat on her. Shun'boo would stand in front of him telling her sister to take their mom out of the room. She would follow behind them walking backwards out of the bedroom so she could see their stepfather at all times if he tried to come behind them are their mom. Shun'boo and her sister help their mom onto the bed asking her was she hurting anywhere. Their mom said, "No" she was not hurting anywhere. Shun'boo looking at her mom to see if she saw any injuries. Their mom told them to help her get cleaned up. Shun'boo went to get a face towel to wash the sweat from her mom face. Shun'boo came back into the bedroom and ask her sister to go and get the blankets off the couch and bring their mom a glass of water to drink. Shun'boo's mom told her when her sister bring the blankets for them both to make a pallet on the floor. Next, they were told to go into the other bedroom and take the covers off the bed and bring them in the bedroom to make another pallet. Her mom said that should be enough room for everybody to lay down.

Her sister came back in the room and gave their mom the glass of water to drink. Shun'boo told her sister that they both had to make two pallets and that they both would lay on one pallet and their other sisters on the other pallet. Their brother could sleep in the bed with their mom. As daylight was breaking in the birds were chirping. Shun'boo closed both of the doors that had an entrance into the bedroom and locked the doors to make sure her mom and siblings were safe. She was hoping her stepfather had calm down. Her mom said for them to lie down and get some rest. They all laid down to try to get some sleep. Shun'boo was awaken from the sound of the telephone ringing. She got up off the floor to go and answer it glancing over at the bed. She didn't see her mom lying in the bed with her brothers. She opened the door to go and see who had call because the telephone had stop ringing as she entered the den. Shun'boo saw her mom and told her that she was about to answer the phone before it had stop ringing. Shun'boo mom said Drea had called and his number was on the caller ID. Shun'boo said, "Ok mom I will call him back. She asked her mom how was she feeling. Shun'boo mom paused for a moment with a facial expression as though she didn't know how to answer the question. Her mom said," I'm alright." Her mom told her to go and wake her next to the oldest sister up so they could cook breakfast. Shun'boo said, "Yes mama." She got the telephone to call Drea back. He said that he was calling to let her know that he had went home to get cleaned up and that he would be over her house in a little while.

She told Drea, ok that she would see him in a little while. Shun'boo went into the bedroom to let her sister know that they had to cook breakfast. All her sisters and brothers were awake. They were all laying down talking. She said, "good morning" to them. Her sister and brother said, "good morning" in a voice like they were tired. Her next to the oldest

CHAPTER 36

However, when her sister and her were done cleaning she told them that she was about to get a bath and get dressed because Drea was on his way over. Shun'boo checked the room to make sure it was clean. She got her bath bag and went to get her bath. She took a quick bath thinking she had to get done. There was a knock on the door and it was her next to the oldest sister letting her know that Drea had arrived. Shun'boo said, "Thank you for letting me know" and could she ask Drea to have a seat in the den area until she was done getting dressed. Her sister told her that Drea was already sitting in the den. Shun'boo ask her sister could she bring her the bathroom cleaning supplies so she could clean the bathroom when she was done bathing. Her sister said, "Yes." She got finish bathing and cleaned the bathroom. She tied her robe up and grabbed the cleaning bucket and her bath bag as she turned the lights off with her hands full. Then she went into the bedroom to finish getting dressed. She ask her baby sister could she take the bathroom cleaning bucket and put it up for her. Her baby sister said, "Yes." Shun'boo told her baby sister that she would treat her to one of her favorite treats. Her baby sister smiling at her took the cleaning bucket to put it up. Shun'boo picked her clothes out, lotion her body, and got dressed. She then turned the curlers on to curl her hair. While she was waiting for the curlers to get hot she applied her makeup. She opened the blinds in the bedroom to get more light to make sure her makeup was on just perfect. After examining her facial makeup, it was perfect.

She closed the blinds and curled her hair. Shun'boo put everything away that she used while getting dressed looking at her entire self once again. She smiled at herself looking in the mirror feeling nice about how she looked. It had been some days since she was able to get fully dress the way she always liked too. Shun'boo went into the den where Drea was. He was so happy to see her his facial expression said it all. He was smiling as some people say, "Ear to Ear." He got up off the couch walking towards Shun'boo reaching his arms out to her in his strong, but gentle arms. She had forgotten about being mad at Drea. He held her close and gentle. Shun'boo was on her tip toes while they hugged each other. She took a deep breathe in and exhale slowly. It was as though Shun'boo was releasing slowly everything bad that had happened to fully receive that which was present. Drea kiss Shun'boo forehead, took her by the hand, and sat on the couch with her. He told her how he had been praying for her and that he missed her and her family. Drea ask Shun'boo was her sister ready to go to the salon to get her hair done. She told him that she should be finish getting dress in a bit. Shun'boo told Drea that she would be right back that she was going to let her mom know that he was there to give the money to her sister to get her hair done. He said, "Ok." Shun'boo knocked on her stepfather and mom bedroom door after they ask who it was. She told them that Drea had come over to bring the money for her sister to get her hair done. Shun'boo mom ask was her sister dress yet so she could take her.

Before Shun'boo could answer her mom, her sister came out the room walking towards her and said, "I'm ready to go get my hair done.

Shun'boo said to her sister "ok" and for her sister to go ask Drea for the money. Shun'boo told her mom that her sister was ready. Her mom said that she would be out shortly to take her sister to the salon. Shun'boo said, "Yes mama I will let her know that you will be out in a bit." Shun'boo went into the bedroom to check and see what her other siblings were doing. They all were getting dressed. She reminded them to clean everything back up and told them that when they were finish getting dress and cleaning up that they would all walk to the store with Drea to get some snacks that they like. Shun'boo went back into the den and her mom was in the kitchen. She told Shun'boo that she had to watch and take care of her baby brother until she get back from dropping her sister off at the Salon. Shun'boo said, "Yes mama." Shun'boo told her sister that her and their siblings was going to get some snacks to eat and take a walk and they would get her something. Shun'boo ask her mom was it alright for them to go with Drea to the store and for a walk. Her mom said, "Yes" She ask her mom could they all go and get something to eat with Drea after her sister come back from getting her hair done. Her mom said, "Yes" that they all could go with Drea except their baby brother because it would be a little too late for him to walk anywhere with them. Shun'boo said, "Thank you" to her mom. Drea smiled at Shun'boo mom and said, "Thank you."

He told her that he would watch and take good care of them all while placing his arms on Shun'boo shoulder standing behind her. Shun'boo knew Drea was happy to spend time with her siblings and her. Drea ask Shun'boo mom would she like anything from the store. Her mom said she would like a cherry coke and a bag of peanuts. Shun'boo mom enjoyed drinking cherry cokes with peanuts poured into her cherry coke. He told her mom that he would buy it for her. Shun'boo mom said, "Thank you' to Drea. Her mom and sister left to go get her sister

CHAPTER 37

He told her he had save some money to buy a car. She ask him why didn't he buy a car. Drea told Shun'boo that he seem to always come across someone who needs, which is more important than him getting a car. He told her that if someone was in need and he had what they needed to help them he would. Drea told Shun'boo when God see that there is a need for him to have a car he would. Drea had told Shun'boo how all the people he had met by walking that if he was driving he probably would have never met them. He told Shun'boo how he enjoyed seeing the elderly sitting on their front porch and how he would speak to them. Also, he had many conversations with people he would meet when walking. Drea told Shun'boo to think about how they both met each other. Drea ask her how did they meet and Shun'boo replied to Drea that we both met each other walking. Drea smiled and said, "yes we did.' He told Shun'boo that he was good and that when he see other people well then he is good. Drea, Shun'boo, and her siblings arrived at the store. Drea told Shun'boo sister's and brother to get enough candy for them because when he finish eating his candy that he would eat some of theirs. Drea laughing as he talked to them. Drea had put Shun'boo baby brother down holding his hand asking him what he wanted. Drea pointing and picking up different snacks for Shun'boo baby brother to choose from. Her baby brother wouldn't say anything to Drea. Shun'boo was trying to get him to say, "yes or no" to Drea or to tell Drea what he wanted. As Drea was asking him what he wanted he pointed at the different snacks with his tiny fragile finger.

He was adorable. Shun'boo loved him. Everyone had picked out what they wanted. Drea asked Shun'boo did she get her sister and mom what they wanted. She said, "Yes." Drea told her that he had picked out a soda to buy for her stepfather. Shun'boo said, "Thank you." Drea spoke to the cashier as they approached the check-out counter. He ask them to put what they had picked out on the counter. The cashier said, 'I see a few of you all seem to enjoy candy. Drea said that he haven't met anyone that doesn't enjoy candy as much as he does. The cashier laughed in a friendly way. She said to Drea that she knew he had a cavity or two. Drea smiled with that gorgeous smile and said to the cashier he never had any cavities. Drea smiling as he told the cashier he guess it pays off by brushing your teeth. They all laughed. Drea said, "Thank you" to the cashier and for her to enjoy the day. Shun'boo and her next to the oldest sister picked up their bags to carry them. Shun'boo ask Drea as they were going out the door of the store did he want her to carry her baby brother back home. Drea said, "No" that he was a Super hero! Shun'boo said, "Yea right." He smiled and pulled Shun'boo close to him and hugged her around the neck. Shun'boo ask Drea was he sure that he didn't want her sister and her to carry their baby brother. Drea said, "No" and if you ask me again you want be able to eat your snacks you got from the store. Drea and Shun'boo laughing at the same time. She said to Drea you are not my dad. He told her "Yes you are right beautiful, but I am older than you."

Shun'boo told Drea alright then you carry him, but remember we told them that we would take a walk around the neighborhood. Drea said, 'Yes, but we are only going to walk around one block from the house." As they approached the neighborhood Shun'boo ask her siblings did they want to get their drinks that they had picked out at the store to drink. They said, "Yes." Shun'boo gave them their Drinks. Drea told Shun'boo let her baby brother drink his juice before they start walking and that way he wouldn't spill the juice on his clothes. Her brother was thirsty. He had drunk the juice halfway. Drea had pulled the juice away from his mouth so he could take a breather between drinking and swallowing properly. Drea said to Shun'boo baby brother "you were thirsty." Drea put her brother down and took one of his hands and started hitting and tapping his hand saying, it was not nice for him to have let him get that thirsty. Shun'boo baby brother must had thought it was so funny for Drea to have spanked himself. They all laughed. Drea picked him up and they began to walk heading towards the house to take a walk around the block from the house. Drea spoke to everyone they passed by and everyone that was sitting outside. They all spoke back in a friendly manner. He always had this inner energy that exuberated love, kindness, laughter, joy and thoughtfulness. Drea loved people and he showed it. Shun'boo watching Drea as they were walking observing his kind mannerism to all people after what Drea had admitted to her about being sexual involved with some other young lady. Shun'boo was mad at the thought, but she didn't want to bring up the matter at that time. Looking at her siblings they all were happy.

They all were talking amongst each other laughing and enjoying the walk. As they sipped their drinks they had finally made it back to the house. Shun'boo thinking to herself that Drea had to go through the side gate to enter to the back door to let them in the house. Drea tried

CHAPTER 38

He said, "Yes." Shun'boo smiled at him. She told him that it was his first time saying anything to Drea that day besides just waving to him to say hi whenever Drea spoke to him. Drea gave him his snacks. Everyone had used the bathroom except Drea. He ask did everyone use the bathroom because he was going to go and use the bathroom. They said, "Yes, we all did." Shun'boo told her siblings to get their snacks out of the bag to eat. She also ask her next to the oldest sister could she put their stepfather and mother sodas in the refrigerator and lay their snacks on the kitchen counter. Drea walked into the den hearing their conversation and ask them did they want to let their stepfather know that he had bought him a soda. Shun'boo said, "No" that she would wait until her mom got back from the salon and give it to him. Shun'boo told them that their mom must have decided to sit and wait for their sister at the salon because she would have been back if she had just dropped her off. Drea told Shun'boo that he was getting ready to leave because he wanted to go and visit his mom as well. Shun'boo ask Drea was he going to call a cab. He said, "No" that he was going to walk to his mom house. It would only take him about a half an hour to get to his mom house from their house. Drea told her brothers and sisters that he was getting ready to leave. They said, "Ok." Drea smiling as usual said to them, "you all are not going to give me a hug before I leave." They all were sitting on the den floor around the television watching music videos. They enjoyed watching that on Saturdays. Drea told them I'm out, be good.

They said, "Ok." Shun'boo walked Drea outside. Drea pulled Shun'boo close to him as he hugged her and kissed her gently on her lips. As he pulled away slowly and gently from her while looking her in the eyes he told her that he was glad to have been able to see her and spend some time with her. He told her he was glad to see her feeling better. Shun'boo turn her face away from Drea as he was speaking to her. Drea took one of his hands and gently held Shun'boo lower face and turned it back towards him. He then told her that he loved everything about her and that she was beautiful inside out. He told her he loved her dearly. He asked Shun'boo to forgive him for hurting her. Shun'boo stood facing Drea looking him in the eyes. She told him that she didn't want to talk about what he had admitted to her because she already had enough to deal with. Drea told her that he understood, but he did want to talk to her. He told Shun'boo that he wouldn't be over to see her Sunday that he was going to rest. Shun'boo said, "Ok." Drea kissed her on the forehead and said, "I will see you later beautiful." Shun'boo went into the house and her siblings were still watching television. Shun'boo heard a knock at the door. Shun'boo looked puzzled thinking who that could be because they didn't get visitors often unless it was her sibling's friends who would come and ask for their brother and younger sister. She peaked out of the blinds to see who was at the door. It was Drea. She opened the door. Drea ask her could she step outside for a minute. She walked outside making sure she closed the door behind her.

She knew her younger sisters would sometime try to listen to Drea and her conversation. Shun'boo ask Drea did he forget something. He said,

"Yes" he sure did. Shun'boo thinking to herself what could it be that he left. Drea reached in his back pocket and took out his wallet and gave her money. He told her that he was so sorry that he promised to take them to get something to eat after her sister got back from the salon. He told Shun'boo to let her siblings know that he couldn't go this time with them to eat, but he would go next time. He told Shun'boo it had slipped his mind that he told his mom that he would come over to visit her and help her with some things around the house. He asked Shun'boo to ask her mom to take them to get something to eat. Drea told Shun'boo that he had given her extra money for gas and for her mom to put it in the car. She said, "Thank you" to Drea. She ask him did he get his candy out of the bag. He told her that he had gotten his candy out of the bag when she had taken her baby brother to use the bathroom when they got back to the house. Drea kiss Shun'boo on the forehead and left. When Shun'boo opened the door she saw her youngest two sisters running from the door. Shun'boo knew that they had been trying to listen to Drea and her. She said to them as they were running to sit down on the den floor that she knew they were standing by the door listening to Drea and her. They both shaking their heads as to say no they weren't. Shun'boo sat on the couch reaching over pulling her baby brother close to her while tickling him.

Shun'boo ask him did he eat all his snacks already. Her next to the oldest sister ask could they quiet down some because one of her favorite music videos was on. Shun'boo said, "Yes." She said to her sister that she was a music video fanatic. Shun'boo laughed because her sister was so focused on the music video. Shun'boo heard a car pull up. She knew that was her sister and mom. She was familiar with the sound of the engine of the car. Shun'boo sister came in the house. Her sister look pretty with her new hair style. She ask them how did they like her hair. They all

CHAPTER 39

Her mom came into the den and told Shun'boo next to the oldest sister to watch her baby brother. She said to Shun'boo she was ready to go. She said, "Yes mama, I have to go get my purse." Her mom said she would be waiting in the car. Shun'boo took the money out of her pocket and put it inside her wallet in her purse. She asked her sisters for one of them to lock the door behind her. They said, "Ok." Shun'boo mom asked her where did they want to eat from. She said to her mom that she wanted to get original and crispy chicken with biscuits and vegetables. Her mom said that they ate chicken a lot. She said to Shun'boo that they should get something else to eat. Shun'boo said that her brothers and sisters enjoyed eating chicken from a restaurant and that she could buy a family meal that would be enough to feed all of them. Her mom told her to make sure she had enough money to buy gas for the car. She said to her mom that Drea had given her enough money. Her mom told her that she wanted to talk to her. Shun'boo sat quietly in the back seat thinking what her mom wanted to talk to her about. They had arrived at the restaurant to place a family order for a chicken meal. Her mother ordered the food. Shun'boo checked the bags to make sure all the food items were in the bag. Her mom asked her was everything in the bag. She said," Yes mama" as they were pulling off from the restaurant. Her mom told Shun'boo that she didn't want to discuss what she wanted to talk to her about while they were at the drive thru.

Her mother told her that her stepfather had told her that while she was sick and out of school she had disrespected him by using sarcastic words. She told her mom that was not true. Her mom told her to shut up because she was insinuating that her stepfather was lying. Shun'boo said to her mom that she was not insinuating anything and that she was just stating the truth. Her mom reached over and slapped her in the face and said to Shun'boo that her stepfather was not lying and she was not going to tolerate her behavior. She told Shun'boo that she was grounded and that she wouldn't be able to see Drea. Shun'boo said to her mom that she was wrong and that every time her stepfather went out she would take her frustration and anger out on her siblings, especially her. Also, if her stepfather told her anything that he didn't like for no reason her mom would ground her from being able to see Drea, but if they both needed money, food, or bills paid they would let her see Drea. However, at times her mom had told her to have sex with Drea because he wouldn't keep giving her money for nothing. Her mom told her to shut up and that she would deal with her later. They had pulled up to the house. She said to Shun'boo for her to get the food bags. Shun'boo got out the car reaching to get the bags and she felt a sharp pain in her chest with a migraine headache. She took a few deep breathes. Her mom yelling telling her to hurry up. Shun'boo trying to hurry up because she didn't want her siblings to see anything. She grabbed the food bags and shut the car door.

Shun'boo followed behind her mom as they went into the house. Shun'boo sat the food bags on the counter and started walking to the bedroom. Her mom call her and told her to wash her hands and fix everyone a plate and leave her stepfather and her food in the containers. Shun'boo mom said to her sisters and brother that they were not allowed to talk to Shun'boo for the rest of the day. Shun'boo finish fixing her sisters and brother's food. She was trying to avoid from making eye contact with them. She didn't want to see the hurt in their eyes. She went to use the bathroom. After she finished using the bathroom and while standing at the sink she looked in the mirror with tears rolling from her eyes thinking to herself how tired she was from all the harsh punishments over the years. She turn the light off and went to the bedroom. She laid across the bed with her room door open. Her chest was hurting extremely bad and felt like a dagger was placed in her chest. Shun'boo laid their taking deep breathes in and out. Her mom came into the bedroom and told her to get up and help her siblings clean the dishes. Shun'boo said, "Yes mama." She went in the kitchen and help with the dishes. It was so quiet. Shun'boo felt the presence of separation that her mom and stepfather had invited in the house. They all were done with cleaning the dishes. Shun'boo went into the bedroom and laid back across the bed. Her next to the oldest sister came in the bedroom behind her and shut the door. Her sister said to her that she knew that Shun'boo was tired as she spoke in a very low voice.

Shun'boo said to her sister that she was alright making sure she spoke in a low voice so that her mom would not hear her. She didn't want her sister to get in trouble. Shun'boo laid there until she drifted off to sleep. When Shun'boo woke up the room was dark and her sisters were all sleep. She looked at them and touched their foreheads. It was her way of saying at that moment she loved them. She went into the kitchen to grab some food that she could put into her hands and eat quickly. She didn't turn on the kitchen light because she didn't want to wake anyone in the house, especially her stepfather and mom. She got a piece of chicken

CHAPTER 40

It was their mom and she said for them to get up and wash their face and brush their teeth. She said to Shun'boo to wake her sisters up with an upset tone in her voice. Shun'boo said, "Yes mama." Her mom said, "I wanted them all to clean out their closet, the dresser drawers, and under the bed. They had to wash both of the bedrooms walls and the laundry room wall. Shun'boo woke her sisters up and told them that they had to get up and wash their face and brush their teeth. They had to get an early start on cleaning up. After everybody had clean up Shun'boo told them what all they had to clean up. Shun'boo younger sister said they were still sleepy. She said to them she knew that they were sleepy and if they all work together they should get it done and they could take a nap later. Shun'boo said to her sister that the four of them would pair up into two of them cleaning up together. They said that sounded good. Shun'boo said two of them would clean the closet and the other two would clean the dresser draws out and everyone would clean under the bed. They were almost done cleaning under the bed when their mom came in the bedroom and told them to come and eat breakfast. They all went to the bathroom to wash their hands. Shun'boo didn't see her brother and youngest sister in their bedroom. She thought that they had to be already eating breakfast. They all finish washing their hands.

Shun'boo being the last one out of the bathroom she turn the light off. They went to the kitchen to eat breakfast. Her sisters and her standing in the kitchen to get their food as their mom fix their plates. Shun'boo mom fixed her plate last.

She had observed her mom had given her a lesser amount of food than her siblings. She thought to herself that this was nothing new. Her mom had done this before. Shun'boo was a bit hungry because she had not eaten dinner, only the chicken she had taken out of the refrigerator. Their mom told them to hurry up because they had a lot to clean. They finish eating. Their mom told them to clean the kitchen up when they were done cleaning everything else up that she had told them too. They all said, "Yes mama." They went to their bedroom and finish cleaning under the bed. They all made the bed up together and Shun'boo next to the oldest sister said she would make two buckets of water for them to wash the walls. As they finish washing the walls of the house the telephone rang and Shun'boo heard her mom answer it. She overheard her mom say that she couldn't talk on the telephone for a couple of days and that she was grounded. Shun'boo knew it was Drea that her mom told she was grounded. Shun'boo said to her sisters that she would empty the water out of the buckets and put them up while they rested. Shun'boo heard her stepfather voice saying why are the dishes still in the sink. Shun'boo went in the den and her mom began yelling telling her to go and get her sisters so that they could get the kitchen cleaned. As Shun'boo was walking to the bedroom to get her sisters they were already coming out of the bedroom. She knew that they had heard their mom yelling. Their stepfather said for them to not half wash any dishes. They all said, "Alright." Their mom said she wanted the kitchen cleaned spotless. After they finish cleaning the kitchen Shun'boo rechecked everything.

Her sisters had already started vacuuming the house. Shun'boo got the bathroom cleaning supplies and cleaned the bathroom. She checked everything to make sure it was clean and turn off the lights. When she came out her sisters had already made up their brother and youngest sister bed. They were finally finish cleaning up. Shun'boo sisters and she were exhausted. They all laid down to take a nap. Shun'boo laid in the bed looking around at her sisters. She knew they were tired. Shun'boo was fighting her sleep. She didn't want to fall asleep on her sisters. One by one they all were fast asleep. She laid there thinking and hoping that her siblings and she could take a nap without their mom waking them up. Shun'boo was awaken by her mom calling her name saying for her to get up and to start getting ready for school. She told Shun'boo she had written an absentee excuse and put the doctor excuse on the dresser. Her sisters woke up except for the middle sister. Their mom told them that they could lay down for another 30 minutes. Shun'boo got up and picked her school clothes out and iron them. She told her sisters she was going to get her bath for school. She reminded her sisters to wake their middle sister up and for them to get up and start preparing for school. Shun'boo got her night clothes and personal bag and went to get her bath. She knew she had to hurry to get a bath. She got done and went to put her things where they belong and clean the bathroom up making sure she turn the light off. She went into the room where her sisters were getting prepared for school. She told them that she left the bathroom cleaning supplies in the bathroom for them to clean up when they got done taking their bath.

Shun'boo said to her youngest baby sister to get the comb and brush so she could braid her hair for school. Everyone had taken their bath for school and iron their school clothes. Shun'boo finish her youngest sister hair. She told her baby sister to get her night clothes and go take

CHAPTER 41

Everyone had eaten and Shun'boo and her next to the oldest sister had clean the kitchen again. Shun'boo turned the kitchen light and dining area lights off. All of her sisters and her brother sat on the couch and the floor watching television. Shun'boo laid her head back and closed her eyes to relax. After relaxing for about thirty minutes she said to her siblings that they should go and used the bathroom because it was close to their bedtime. Shun'boo walked her baby brother to her stepfather and mother bedroom and knocked on the door. Her mom asked who was knocking. Shun'boo said to her mom that it was her knocking and that she had fed her baby brother. Her mom opened her bedroom door and got her baby brother. She told Shun'boo for them to turn the television off and get in the bed so they will be ready for school tomorrow. Shun'boo made sure her brother and her youngest sister had used the bathroom. After she ask them did they use the bathroom and they assured her they did. She turned their bedroom light off and went in the den to make sure the television was turned off too. She checked all the doors to make sure they were locked. Shun'boo went and laid down. She thought about school and all the makeup class work she would have to complete. As she was in her thoughts she drifted off to sleep. While sleeping she had the dream again. She dream she was falling into a deep dark hole and someone grabbing her securely and bringing her back out of the hole safely never letting her hit the bottom. Shun'boo woke up to the birds chirping. She got up to start her day. As she was stretching she was smiling at the sound of the birds chirping.

Shun'boo truly enjoyed hearing the sounds of birds even watching them fly and maneuver through the sky. Birds appeared to Shun'boo to be free not bound up. They appeared to be cared for and taken care of. She thought about this scripture she had read in her bible (Matthew 6:26) as she woke up her siblings for school. As she went to the bathroom to brush her teeth and freshen up there was a knock on the bathroom door. She heard her next to the oldest sister say open the door because she had to use the bathroom. Shun'boo opened the door. Her sister asked her how did she feel about going to school after being absent for a few days knowing she had to do make up work. Shun'boo smiled at her sister and said to her sister that she had thought about it. Shun'boo said that hopefully her teachers would be nice to her. Shun'boo reminded her sister to turn the light off when she come out of the bathroom. Shun'boo went into the bedroom to finish getting dress. As she was getting dressed she ask her other sisters did they need any help with anything. They all ask her for something of hers to wear. She said, "Yes." Her youngest sister said to Shun'boo since she couldn't fit her clothes could she wear a pair of her stud earrings. Shun'boo said, "Yes." Shun'boo mom yelled for her youngest sister to come where she was. Shun'boo said to her next to the oldest sister to hurry up and finish curling her hair so that it won't be too late to catch the bus. Shun'boo checked her hair and got the excuse her mom had written and the doctor excuse. She put both of them inside her book bag. Shun'boo got her purse and gave all her sisters' money.

She ask her middle sister to give their brother the money. She would give it to him when they left out for school. Shun'boo next to the oldest sister said she was ready to leave for school. Their mom came into the room yelling at them to clean the top of the dresser off in their bedroom. Shun'boo mom ask her did she give her brother and sisters money. Shun'boo said, "Yes mama." Her mom ask her to give her the money. Shun'boo thinking to herself what money was her mom talking about. Shun'boo mom told her to stop looking confused like she didn't know what she was talking about. She thought that her mom was talking about the extra money Drea had given to her to buy gas for her stepfather car. Shun'boo went into her purse and got a generous amount of money for her mom to put gas in the car. Shun'boo mom started yelling at her saying she think she is grown. Her mom told her she didn't decide how much money to give her for gas. She said to her mom that she had given her enough to fill the car up and have money left over. Her mom told her to shut up and to give her all the money Drea had given to her. Shun'boo said to her mom that it was not right for her to take the money Drea had given her. She said to her mom that she made sure Drea got her sister hair done. Also, Drea had given her money to treat them to dinner. Her mom kept yelling shut up. Shun'boo said, "Mom I also gave my siblings money to last them for the week." Shun'boo mom said since you won't shut up I will shut your mouth for you. Shun'boo mom started walking towards her. Shun'boo already knew her mom was going to hit her.

As her mom was walking towards her Shun'boo asked her mom what did she say and do wrong. Her mom slapped her repeatedly in the face. Her sister was yelling for their mom to stop. Shun'boo put her hands up to try to block her mom from the slaps, and strikes on her head. Shun'boo broke loose from her mom and ran out the house. While

CHAPTER 42

Shun'boo asked her sister did she see a scratch on her face because her face was stinging. Her sister said, "Yes" she had a visible long scratch in her face. Her sister ask her what was she going to do to try to cover it up. Shun'boo said to her sister that she had makeup in her purse to cover it up. She told her sister that she was worried about her teachers asking for her an absentee excuse that she had put into her book bag before her sister told them to hurry up and use the restroom because the first school bell had already rung. Shun'boo sister told her after she had used the restroom and washed her hands that she was going to go ahead to the locker, get her books for class, and she would see her later. Shun'boo knew her sister was concerned about her. She had seen the concern for her through her sister's eyes. Shun'boo said to her sister that she loved her and she would see her later. Shun'boo took a napkin and wet it and clean the scratch on her face. She got her foundation make-up out of her purse that she very seldom use. She had bought it to cover up a scrape she had gotten while racing with her next to the oldest sister. As Shun'boo was putting on her make-up she saw the girl through the restroom mirror who had ask her about Drea. Shun'boo finish applying the foundation make-up on her face. The girl walked up to the sink beside Shun'boo. The girls that were in the bathroom started laughing Shun'boo thinking to herself that she didn't want to get in and altercation with the girls or either of her friends. Shun'boo thought that if they wanted to fight her that indeed they would need to be taken to the alter for healing.

Shun'boo thought she was in no mood for their mess. She was already frustrated with what happened between her mom and her earlier. As Shun'boo was leaving out the bathroom the girl who had confronted her about Drea said to her that she see somebody have already beat you up. Shun'boo turned around and said to her, "What did you say to me?" The girl said, "You heard me." The girl was walking up to Shun'boo saying she was about to beat her. There was "No" fear in Shun'boo. The girl punched Shun'boo in the face and Shun'boo tore into her like a lion devouring their prey. She and the girl were fighting in the bathroom. Shun'boo could feel the other girls and see them trying to pull them apart. The fight went outside the restroom and into the hallway across from the school office. Shun'boo saw her sister. She heard the school announcements being spoken over the intercom. Her sister ran up and started hitting the girl. Some teachers had grabbed Shun'boo trying to hold her. Shun'boo was tussling with them. Shun'boo could hear them yelling for help for someone to go get the principal. Shun'boo saw her sister and the girl fighting. She broke away from the teachers who were trying to hold her and ran behind the girl and grabbed her. Shun'boo pushed her into the school's glass trophy case and glass shattered. Shun'boo felt someone grab her from the back and pick her up and it was the principal. He was yelling for the other male teacher to get Shun'boo sister and the girl. The principal had locked Shun'boo arms from the back taking her into the office. Shun'boo could see the other male teachers bringing her sister and the girl into the office. The girl was still tussling with the teachers.

She got a loose from the teacher and reached for the paper hole puncher and threw it at Shun'boo sister. The principal told Shun'boo to sit in the chair and not to come out. As soon as he shut the door Shun'boo open the door and took the flag pole and tried to stick the girl with the pointed end of the flag pole. The principal grabbed Shun'boo cuffing her arms behind her while yelling for the other school administrators to call the police. The principal took Shun'boo out of the office. While standing in the hallway the teachers were trying to get the students to go to their classes. Everyone was trying to see what had conspired. The principal took Shun'boo to a detention room on the second floor of the school. The principal called security to come to the detention room. When security arrived they had Shun'boo sister. They told them both to sit in a chair. Shun'boo hugged her sister. The principal said for them not to touch each other. The principal said to the security personnel for them to both stay with Shun'boo sister and her and that he was going to the office to call their mom. Shun'boo and her sister sat there quiet. Shun'boo was furious as she thought to herself that she never picked or bothered anyone. The girl picked the wrong day to have instigated a fight with her. The detentions room door open and it was a police officer and the principal. They came in and the officer said to Shun'boo sister and her that they were being transported to the juvenile detention facility. The officer asked Shun'boo to stand up and place her hands behind her back. The police officer placed hand cuffs on her wrist. The detention room door opened and it was another officer.

He ask Shun'boo sister to stand up and place her hands behind her back and the officer put hand cuffs on her too. They lead them out of the school to the police cars. Shun'boo sister and her were put into separate police cars and taken to the juvenile detention facility. When they arrived they searched them and took them in this room where the walls were built out of bricks and question them about what had happened at school. Shun'boo sister and she only answered the questions the officers ask them. After the officers had finish asking them both questions they placed Shun'boo sister and her in two separate rooms. There was a huge glass inside the rooms they were put in and they could see each other. The police officer ask Shun'boo to have a seat in one of the chairs. The officer shut the steel door and locked it. Shun'boo heard the officer pull on the door to ensure the door was securely locked. Shun'boo and her sister looking at each other through the glass mirror. Shun'boo said to her sister she loved her. She was hoping her sister could read her mouth and know what she had said. Her sister said she loved Shun'boo too. Shun'boo heard the voice of a person over the intercom saying no talking at all. Shun'boo saw a police officer come into the room. They had her sister escorted out of the room. Shun'boo was thinking where is the police officer taking her sister. Shun'boo thought did they take her sister to another room because she had said to her sister she loved her. Shun'boo heard the door unlock in the room she was placed in. A police officer said to Shun'boo that her parent was there to get her sister and her. The officer asked Shun'boo did she want to use the restroom.

She said, 'Yes." Shun'boo thought to herself what was going to happen once they got back to their house. Shun'boo finish using the restroom and washed her hands. Shun'boo reached to turn the light off and realized she was at a juvenile detention facility. Shun'boo thought as she was walking down the long hallway being escorted by the police officer. She had been so conditioned into a pattern of making sure she always turned the lights off at her house because of the rage her stepfather and mother would have if they left a light on. The police officer took Shun'boo in the room where her mom and sister were. Shun'boo mom was filling out a paper. After she had finished the officer said to their mom that she would be notified by mail when the court date would be. Shun'boo sister and she walked behind their mom to the car. As their mom was driving out of the parking lot Shun'boo's mom started yelling at her sister and her blaming everything on Shun'boo. Her mom saying that Shun'boo had gotten her sister in trouble. She said to Shun'boo she was the blame for what had happened earlier that morning. She told Shun'boo she was grounded. Shun'boo trying to hold back her tears as they fell onto her lap like clouds releasing its water of rain on the earth. She thought who would help her or be a voice for her since she chose to silence her own voice because of the thought of being separated from her family; she loved unconditionally.

ABOUT THE AUTHOR

Roshonda Alexander is the author of This Happens. Roshonda was born September 21, 1975 in Alabama. She is the oldest child, and she has six younger siblings. In a household that size including her stepfather, and mother could be challenging, at times with all the different personalities. She loves her family dearly even in their indifference.

Roshonda is a natural caregiver. She loves people and always had a concern about people well-being. She was a giving child, sharing with others. Even until this day, those unique God-given traits still abides in her heart. She serves in her community and enjoys it. Her heart's desire is to see this generation and the next generations maximize all their gifts to the fullest. She hopes that people will help someone else who cross their path. Roshonda hopes that this book will help restore healing to the abused by the love and grace of God. She hopes that the abused will choose to forgive. Roshonda also hopes that this book will help the abuser to seek God for the root cause of them to have begun to be an abuser, seeking God, and whom they abused for forgiveness. She also hopes the abusers forgive themselves, and that they be renewed with a new mind-set and heart. There is God's grace for the abuser as well as forgiveness.

Printed in the United States
By Bookmasters